3EARTH

Two Earths, one race for time.

By Brooks A. Agnew

SOON TO BE A MAJOR MOTION PICTURE

If you're not a good reader, don't worry about it. I read it for you. Buy this book, and I will send the free download of the entire book in audio simply by writing me at bearthfan@x2-radio.com with your purchase receipt number. That's it. Free!

Brooks Agnew

Table of Contents

Foreword

Virtually every ancient civilization records their version of the formation of planet Earth. They also speak of a universal flood. And no matter what age from which these ancient races spoke of their version of the future, they all looked to this day. The twenty-first century was a time when there would be a grand division; a separation of the light from the darkness that would judge the Earth.

Modern civilization decries this tradition. Our planet has been accessed by nearly every current society by air travel, high speed internet, and global communications. We can meet and know of other peoples around the globe any time we like. There are fewer secrets and fewer mysteries. That is to say, the pyramids have been studied and those studies are available for everyone to read. The Bermuda Triangle has been filmed from beneath the surface, and those films are available for all to see with unfettered access. The impossible architecture of the Yucatan has been explored and explained from every possible viewpoint, and we are free to make up our own minds how those ancient engineers moved and carved and fitted stones of immovable weight and size without so much as a wheel.

But there is still a mystery that remains unsolved. Or at least, the data that we have in hand seems to indicate an origin that we cannot accept as a people. It is clear now that we did not crawl forth from some primordial ooze. In all of our studies of fruit flies, bacteria, primates, and fowl throughout the entire process of natural selection, there is not a single example of one species jumping to another. There are no fish that become birds. There are no dogs that become horses. There are no reptiles that develop warm blooded, upright walking bodies.

So, what about creation? How did all these species come to be? As though that was not enough to boggle the mind, it is the presence of man that presents the greatest question. Sentient and full of spirit, how did man come to be?

Well, by the time a reader makes his way through a few books of Genesis, he is introduced to no fewer than 5 races of sentient beings, none of whom are from Earth. Gods, serpents, lower man, higher man, and Nephilim and their offspring are all explained, but their origin is not. Lower man is brought to Earth to till the ground. Higher man is made from the dirt of the Earth, and has the breath of life instilled in him by God. A thousand years later, his DNA is used to create a breedable female that is birthed by a surrogate mother on another world, raised to young adulthood, and brought to Earth at the end of the 6th Day of creation.

Then what happens? Well, according to the ancient records, mankind begins to divide himself into two ideologies. One race, the descendants of Adam's breeding with Eve, wants to follow God and try as much as possible to be like Him, so that they can know Him. They are a creative race full of mercy, and they spontaneously obey the laws out of mercy and a longing for liberty and peace. To these people, the Earth is like heaven with challenge and room for growth.

The other race, the descendants of Lucifer's encounter with Eve, seeks to destroy the other race and consume every ounce of bounty that they have created. They create nothing. Nations that allow this race to proliferate are plunged into turmoil, mayhem, and can be viewed from space as a dusty and unkept barnyard. Where there is a fence between them, it is easy to see one side is lush and groomed and full of color and life and music and art. The other side is dark at night. It's streets are littered with windblown trash. The canals from its rivers are full of dead animals and trash and sewage, because there is no room in their minds for anything but rage and jealousy and hatred. To these people, Earth is like hell. It is torture and conflict, betrayal and mistrust. It is a massive movement ready to swarm over the Earth like locusts waiting for the right signal from nature to do so.

If it is green, they want it to wither and die for want of water or to be trampled under the feet of soldiers or the refugees they generate. If it is alive, they want to enslave it, rape it, and eventually find a reason to kill it. They follow a dark and sadistic imaginary deity by which they justify their lifestyle. They know the higher race will generate more than enough for them to consume. And they know they can defecate where they sleep, and urinate where they eat, and as long as they die in the battle to kill infidels, they will be transported to heaven with great reward.

The planet Earth is much like the people upon it. There are two races of people with different energies. There are two Earths as well. The higher Earth had the Adamic race upon it up to the generation of Noah. It was a higher energy, some call spiritual energy. The lower Earth had the generations of Lucifer. It was made of a lower energy, some call temporal energy.

During the Flood, these two Earths were merged. Like the human body, merged with a spirit, is two types of energy occupying the same space at the same time, the Earth is made of these two energies occupying the same space in space and time.

One day, they will come apart, just as the spirit leaves the body when its time in mortality is done. That day is upon us. That day, foreseen by every ancient race, is now. This book is the true story with some characters and some action, but nevertheless true. The characters are representative, but they are real. Every effort has been made to entertain, but also to leave you with the lesson that is true.

3

All those races from the book of Genesis are here, once again. The struggle for dominance and control of the creation of man and the Earth is real, and both sides are playing by rules and for keeps. Billions of souls are at stake. Planet Earth is the center battle of the universe, according to the ancient record. The results of this war between light and darkness will affect the entire universe. There is nowhere for you to hide. There is no escape. You chose to be here at this time for a reason. This book will make you aware of that reason again. Hopefully, it will do it before it is too late.

Chapter 1

The room was cool, but that did not stop the sweat. It was 3:30 in the morning, again. Richard Daring was awake, flipping his pillow over so he didn't have to sleep on the wet spot. He had crashed again. The dual engine cart he was driving, in his dream, was traveling at more than 120 miles an hour as he streaked past dozens of single engine carts on the straightaway toward the front of the pack.

It was the way these races were arranged. The fans liked to see the difference between the faster, twin-engine carts and the slower, single-engine carts. It was like watching Indy cars race against go-carts. Well, they were all go-carts, but it was sophisticated now. They ran on Methanol and sported complex suspensions that allowed them to hug the asphalt like a shadow. One man, and one cart, acted like a single mass stuck to the curves so tightly that it was difficult to breathe as the force of the body against the harness holding it in the seat was many times the force of gravity.

That is until something lifts the wheel from the asphalt. Open wheel vehicles have their hot and sticky tires exposed to the barriers like the wall and the hay bales that line the curvy carting course. They are also exposed to other hot and sticky tires. And when two tires touch one another at more than 100 miles an hour, the one behind is ripped from its grip of the asphalt and forced into the air, where it has no business being.

The cart will immediately travel in a straight line by the laws of physics perpendicular to the origin of force. Like an iron ball breaking the rope from which it is suspended while being slung around a central point, the cart will head outward, unfettered, until it is stopped by an immovable object.

Richard, the racing community called him Dick, and his glistening orange, twin-engine cart slammed into the high wall and left a 200 foot long black mark in what seemed like a single second to the cameras. The instant replay would become iconic in the racing world. The agony of defeat. But, the replay in Dick's memory was slow and twisted. His breath, quickened by the shock of being launched upward into the air, was cut off as he braced and gripped the wheel while he blinked once, twice before striking the wall.

He thought again and again about the impact. The wall wiped his right front wheel and spindle and its entire brake system off the cart like a twig disappears in the path of weedeater. His head snapped against the helmet tether, designed to keep his neck from breaking on just such an impact, holding his head in just the right position for the wall to grind away at his helmet. Shards of lexan and fiberglass exploded against his nomex covered cheeks, and into his right eye.

He jerked awake. Again he had wished to turn his face, or to shut his eyes. Again, he had let up a little on the throttle to miss the youngster's tire next to him. Again, he had tried to avoid that crash, and sometimes he could almost do it. Still, every time he shot back into consciousness, awake in his night sweat, his right eye was still dark. It sparkled sometimes as the nerves would strain to see again, but it was always dark.

And so was his racing career. He could not get certified to race again with only one eye. So he did other things. Oh, he didn't work at a fast food place or as someone else's mechanic. He did, however, find other ways to, well, compete.

Chapter 2

"I like the way you say shifting," Yuki said as she brushed her little white hand across Dick's bare arm as it rested on his car window sill. She was bouncing from car to car trying to give the streaming audience an introduction to all the drivers and all the cars.

Pasadena was always a car town. Songs were written about it. The whole culture of America seemed to revolve around the automobile for two generations. And this street, Colorado Boulevard, was the iconic strip of straight asphalt and stop lights that seemed to embody the entire art.

Yuki was part of the new generation of fans who believe that there is a substitute for cubic inch. That is to say, size does not necessarily matter. She was small, at just 4 feet 11 inches and barely 90 pounds, but she was no trifle in the underground racing industry. She had started a business with the perfect match between three, high energy phenomena.

Part of her business was online gambling, hooking thousands of high rolling people from all over the world who like to bet on just about anything. Part of it was the high-tech camera business, with cameras mounted on the car, in the car, on the driver, and even in the air with zippy little drones that could follow a car up to 140 miles an hour. She took the audience along for the ride of their lives.

The final ingredient of Yuki's online gambling racing empire was that the cars were real. The drivers were real. The streets and the dangers of pedestrians, other cars, and police were real. The money these drivers competed for was real, and it attracted the best of the best from all around the world to compete.

The tension was surreal, as these little cars with one, two or three turbochargers sucked in cold California air and crunched it up to three atmospheres mixed with high-octane fuel or various blends of alcohol, and shoved into a combustion chamber where it would convert an engine designed for high-mileage commuting into a screaming, computer chipped monster that spits asphalt out the back of a car.

All of these racers liked their lives and their music a certain way; loud and dangerous. It was sexy and extremely profitable. It was also highly illegal and a target of a multi-agency investigation to bust the drivers, the gamblers, and the little girl who ran it all.

Yuki had a headset mike with an earpiece that allowed her to stay connected to the central hacker. Kramer is called a hacker, because he was a hacker. As a middle schooler, he cracked his way into the California State DOT, and made the headlines doing so. He was a minor, so did little time in the juvenile court system, but the probation terms were brutal. No internet. No association with other hackers. And, no computer access until he was 21.

Okay. He was 21. He could do as he pleased, and what pleased him was to associate with his best friend, Dick Daring. He learned to write fuel management code for the systems that utilize high-compression turbochargers attached to motors that had no business being turbocharged. He also knew how to hack the traffic control systems and alter the lighting and flow of traffic. And, in a little chat window on the side of his screen, he would send and monitor the laptop text screens of Pasadena police cars.

These were essential skills for a person in charge of mapping and facilitating a street race. The lights along the race are turned to green. The police cars are slowly, meticulously sent messages that lead the police cars far away from the race's roadway. Dispatch calls to the cars are monitored by team mates who alert the central command of any possible complaints or calls for pursuit. The race would only last for three or four minutes anyway. In that amount of time, the cars could cover 6 miles or more, making it nearly impossible for any type of roadblock to be set up. They had been racing for nearly two years, and except for a harmless crash or two, the business was going great and ready for franchising.

There were spotters, who were positioned around the race circuit to report by radio any crashes, stalls, or possible police interruptions. Other team members would contact thousands of gamblers across the globe and let them know the time, but never the place of the race. The FBI was monitoring these networks as well. They might even be posing as gamblers. They knew the time, but they never knew the place or the route of the race.

As the evening grew into night, and the pool of global cash grew with an intensity only equaled to watching a new kind of bomb detonate on live TV, the cars arrived in the Pasadena City College parking lot. Some were dark and low to the ground, humming with nearly open pipes to make way for the ultra-compressed fuel and air that would be roaring through its custom stainless steel exhaust system.

Others were nearly stock looking on the outside. Sleepers. Quiet and unassuming, they acted like stealth racers. They looked like the neighbor's car, but once the throttle was pressed forward toward the front grill, the turbos would kick in, and more than one thousand horsepower would seek to rip the rubber off the front rims, yanking the car forward against its will to speeds greater than 140 miles an hour. Many a Lamborghini had been sent home crying while attempting to paddle shift past one of these little rocket ships.

Daring's car was a glistening black Honda. Okay, he liked American muscle more than anything, but for this type of racing the car had to be like a cart. It had to be light, agile, and yet be able to hold onto a power plant that was trying to leap through the front grill. It required special engineering and high strength steel and carbon fiber. It required special fuel, laced with an octane coupled with high strength magnets long the coiled fuel lines to upgrade the combustion reaction. It required a dynamic chip code that altered the fuel mixture every 50 RPM, giving the cylinder everything it could possibly contain before exploding and then exiting through the highly polished exhaust valves and around the blades of the turbocharger that would make it go even faster. It was like an uncontrolled chain reaction all the way to 12 thousand RPM, generating more horsepower than the two-wheel dyno at the college could measure. It was faster than a twin-engine go-cart.

Yuki's little Catholic school skirt flipped precociously as she bounced in front of the shoulder camera held by one of her crew. "Okay racers and fans, I hope your wagers are all locked in. We are only minutes away from the green hanky!"
"Yeah. Too bad there is no American muscle here tonight. That will be fun," yelled Dick out his car window at Yuki.
"I like the way you say muscle," she twerked as she skipped along in front of the cars now lining up. She waved a green scarf in front of the camera and spun around like a little dervish, intoxicating her global fan base. She acted like she could hear the applause from thousands of men sitting in their underwear, cheering at their computer screens or tablets as she locked her eyes with each of theirs through the camera's lens directly to their souls.

The look was long enough to make the heart race, but short enough to make you reach for the screen to touch her just for a moment. Her dark eyes were enhanced with perfect makeup and the camera light made them shine like onyx against her porcelain skin framed by recently trimmed jet black bangs and long, flowing silk sheets of hair that reached past the bottom of her white school girl blouse tucked into the very short blue plaid skirt.

They couldn't help themselves. The men. They bet sometimes thousands of dollars on a car or two they thought might win the night's totally illegal competition, but it was the illegal fantasies they had about Yuki that made her business the richest of its kind in the world. No one could duplicate what she had built. They knew the time; they just didn't know the place.

Chapter 3

"We're here to see professor Wesson." Said Smith.

"It's Doctor Wesson. Not professor, yet. The asshole dean won't let her advance. And she's not here. Who wants to know?" Bett said with a sharpness that meant she was ready to fight.

"We're with the U.S. Secret Service," said Smith, gesturing to his partner, also dressed in a dark suit and tie and sunglasses.

"Huh. Men in black. Right." She said.

"I thought you guys protected the president. What do you want with the boss?" asked Rhino, the other of Dr. Loretta Wesson's grad students. He was large, even for a Samoan.

"We do. We also work for the US Treasury. But today, we work for the president," said Jones. He was the same height as Smith but more slight of build. Smith looked like a solid man with a clean jaw, dark hair, and a crease so sharp in his pants it looks like he never sat down. He reminded Rhino of Steve Smith, the quarterback for San Francisco. He saw him up close once at the end of a game. He was courteous as he congratulated him for trying to beat them. He was built the same way as Smith.

"So, is the president here?" asked Rhino.

"We can't tell you where the president is, but we must speak with Dr. Wesson immediately. Do you know where we can find her? And remember, lying to us is against the law," said Smith.

"We're not telling you shit until you tell us what you're doing here," shot Bett directly into Smith's face with the addition of a pointed finger. She didn't quite touch him, but she wanted to. He wasn't fooling her. She noticed a pen in his pocket and bored into him even more.

"I know all about you guys. That pen is probably some sort of weapon, and you make people disappear that you don't like. You taking us to Guantanamo, Smith? Everyone knows it's all corrupt." She was frustrated, and wanted to argue.

Smith stood still, didn't change his expression of calm one bit, and asked again. "When can we speak with Dr. Wesson.?"

"Hold on." She turned toward the office door attached to the waiting area where they stood. She had to make a call. "Keep an eye on them Rhino."

"You da man." He stepped forward and folded his arms. Smith was about six feet tall, but Rhino was about nine inches taller and outweighed Smith by at least 100 pounds. He used to be a gifted running back. His upper body was still fast and powerful. His leg, well that is another story.

Rhino was a major draft choice for the pros. He even played a pre-season game once in San Francisco. He earned the nickname, because he scored so many touchdowns by blasting the defensive line backward over the goal line. He could push three linemen once he got going. He was going to turn pro his Sophomore year, but then sometimes plans change. He was struck by a car that slid out of control during a California rain. It was a Land Rover.

The press couldn't leave it alone, as the accident shattered his lower right leg. The doctors put it back together where he could walk fine, but his running days were over. "The Land Rover can take the charge of a rhino, but the Rhino couldn't take the charge of the Land Rover," they quipped on nearly every sports talk show in the country. His football days turned into physics days. He graduated with honors, and is now on a PhD track working with Dr. Wesson on planetary core geology.

Bett acted and spoke like a man. She wore leather when she could, but wore men's jeans and kept her hair greased back. She detested men. They were unhealthy and messy and had no regard for a woman's heart. So she would have no regard for theirs. She took martial arts, but mostly for the kick boxing and getting to spar with men. She liked hitting them. She tried smoking, because it made her unapproachable, but her focus on being lean and healthy was harshed by the whole idea of smoking.

She rode a Harley and hadn't dated anyone since she was an undergraduate. There was only seating for one on the bike, and that said enough to everyone around her about her social life. Cal Tech was a pathway where she could use her brains and determination to be successful without a man. It pissed her off to no end that Dean Russell wouldn't allow Dr. Loretta Wesson become a full professor. It had been long enough. She had the right stuff, and her thesis was kickass.

And now these men in black. Secret Service. Bull shit.

Chapter 4

Dr. Loretta Wesson was just like her engineer father. Oh, she was a daddy's girl, but her favorite subject was geology. Shortly after her mother passed away, while Loretta was only 9, there was an earthquake in the valley where they lived. It seemed like it lasted for a minute or two, but probably it was much shorter than that. At first, it was frightening, because there was nowhere to go to get away from it. Unless you could jump in the air and stay there, there was nothing you could do but wait it out.

Her heart raced for hours after that quake. There were aftershocks for days. She was hooked for life. She had to know what caused them, how to predict them, and whether other planets had them as well. When the US Geological Survey read her thesis they were fascinated with her theories and advanced her a grant to work at Cal Tech to help with her studies. Cal Tech was not so excited about the prospect. A new theory of planetary core geology that was radical could possibly embarrass the institution. They expressed caution.

Perhaps they would talk to Dr. Russell, the dean of geology. Stan Russell had always had a crush on Loretta, but he was overweight and she didn't really smile at him the right way. He grew a beard to kind of cover up his fat neck, but it came in red. He kept it. It made him feel more secure, because Loretta couldn't see his skin. He was incredibly smart and well published, but his aversion to being touched, or to having someone see him, or really just to see his skin, made him avoid crowds.

Usually it wasn't a problem. Geology was not a crowd sport. He could write papers, and his peers would approve of his armchair methods, because most of them were just rock doctors anyway. They dug with hand shovels or drills, but they really didn't know better than anyone else how the planet

15

was constructed on the inside. And to have an associate professor, even if it was at Cal Tech, introduce a new theory might be a little too much. Too risky. People would stare in their direction.

So Stan, he like her to call him Stan, would be nice and smile under his auto-darkening thick glasses and through his red beard, and perhaps next year the board of Regents would approve her full professorship. He would fold his hands together at the end of his long sleeves, always snapped at the cuff, never rolled up. He would glance away, even though his thick glasses made it impossible to see his eyes, because the energy of her connecting with his eyes was like being naked. It scared the hell out of him.

Loretta was jogging, as she always did in the cool California mornings. She had no class load before noon, and rarely made the office before 10 AM. She had great grad students who could answer any textbook problems or help students with research in the physical chemistry lab. There was a slight, San Gabriel fog on the sidewalks that morning as she made her way along the divided road near her house in San Marino. The road was divided by a wide center island that was grassy with maple trees groomed along the way. The grass was soft and spongy, making it easy on the knees, and the cars were far enough away on either side to keep it safe.

San Marino was a very safe neighborhood. It has only a couple of retail locations in the small city of mostly millionaires. They didn't want anyone from outside coming to San Marino to shop for anything, so the prices were about 10-20% higher than in Pasadena or San Gabriel. It worked. Locals, mostly. She wore a jogging suit rather than sweats. It wouldn't be appropriate in this neighborhood for sweats. Runners keep their heads down, mostly. The ritzy neighbors walked their ritzy dogs on this same grass strip.

16

Her cell phone rang. Normally, she would never take a call while she was jogging, but something told her to at least take a look to see who it was. Could be an emergency. Dad was getting older.

Bett. I told her not to..."Hello? Bett, I told you I..."

"Dr. Wesson," she interrupted. She never called her Dr. Wesson unless it was in public, "there are some men here to see you." Bett used her male staccato voice.

"Well, take a message," she said with a slight puff to her voice. "I am running, and I won't be there for at least an hour. Have Rhino.."

"No. These guys say they're from the secret service. They say they work for the president and they want to talk to you. I think it's bull shit, but honestly, they look like the real deal."

"The secret service? What the hell could...okay. I'm turning down my street. I'll do a quickie shower and be there in 30. Hold tight."

"Right on."

Bett dropped her cell phone into the right pocket of her jeans and opened the door from Loretta's office into the geology office waiting area. Smith and Jones were still there. Still standing at nearly attention. "Smith and Jones? Like those names are real. Seriously, tell the truth." Bett said.

They both reached for their badges and held them out for Bett to see. "Well, damn'" she said, stretching the last word out like a southern redneck. "Dr. Wesson said she'll be here in 30. Can we get you something to drink?"

"No ma'am. We're fine." Said Jones.

"Ma'am? Jesus, Joe Friday. My mother was ma'am. I am Bett Dyson. Just call me Bett."

"Okay, Bett." Smith quipped. "Listen, we are kind of in a hurry. Our ride is outside taking up a few parking spaces. Is there any way you can..."

"Cool your jets, cowboy." Bett stepped forward ready to get physical. She pointed her finger at Smith's chest and nearly poked him with it. He didn't change his expression at all. Motionless. "You come in here with this bull shit secret service story, which I still don't buy, and make these demands. Are we under arrest or something? 'Cuz if we're not, then you shut the hell up and wait."

"You're not under arrest," said Jones. "There is an emergency, for which Dr. Wesson is uniquely qualified to help the president."

"Help the president?" asked Rhino. "What do you mean help the president? He needs my help, I'm suiting up."

"Put your helmet down, Rhino," said Bett. "What kind of help?"

"It would be best if we explain this to Dr. Wesson. I have a feeling we need to make room for three," said Smith.

"Yes sir," said Jones. He turned way, lifted his wrist to his mouth, and mumbled to the ears on the other end, "Three and some boxes of records. Copy that."

Chapter 5

I'm a geologist, she reasoned. What the heck could the secret service want with geologist? Her hair was still wet, but the warming California air felt good through the sunroof of her little Ford. It was new, and got incredible mileage, but she really wanted a Cadillac. Not one of the big ones. She wanted the CTS or something like that. They had the zip of kind of a sports car with the prestige of a full professor. Once she was promoted, and had tenure, she'd buy one. Then she could be sure. Not many jobs out there for geologists.

She turned into the PCC parking lot to cut through to Cal Tech. "Holy shit," she said out loud. What the hell is a helicopter doing in the parking lot? And there are two uniformed people in it. She accelerated past the auto shop area and bounced over the speed bumps to enter the Cal Tech parking area. Zipping around the back, she arrived just outside her office area. Bett's motorcycle was parked in the second slot. Hers was reserved.

She jogged into the building and down the hall to the geology office and into the waiting area. It looked like a standoff. "Rhino. Morning. Bett, what's up?"

"This is agents Smith and Jones. I still don't believe that, but they say they're here because the president needs your help."

"The president? What can I do? How can I help?" she said folding her arms. Damn. Body language. She unfolded her arms.

"Dr. Wesson, we need you to come with us and bring your evidence on the thesis you submitted on planetary core geology," said Smith. "We are prepared to accommodate your two graduate students as well, if you don't mind."

She looked at Bett and then at Rhino. "Ready?" she quizzed. They nodded. "I'll show you which boxes. Rhino, give a hand."

They gathered up 8 record boxes full of notebooks, photographs, charts, and two laptop computers. They shuffled out of the door like they were expecting a fire alarm to go off. Once outside, they had a 200 foot walk to the edge of the building. Once they reached the edge of the building, they could see into the Pasadena City College parking lot.

"What the hell is that?" asked Bett almost out of breath from the effort to carry that box so far.
"That is a modified Sikorsky UH-60 Black Hawk helicopter with stealth technology," said Rhino. "I saw it on Discovery Channel."
"Very good, Rhino," said Smith.
"You da man," said Rhino with a smile on his face like a little kid getting ready to ride a roller coaster.
"Well, it's a lot bigger than they look on TV," said Bett.

They soon reached the helicopter. The side of the helicopter opened hydraulically as they approached. The pilot and copilot were already warming the turbines, and the pitch was annoying to the ears. They handed the boxes to Rhino, who stacked them under direction of agent Jones. Smith jumped up into the bay and reached down for Bett, pulling her up into the helicopter and then reached for Loretta. Rhino placed his hands on the floor of the helicopter and lifted himself into the craft. Smith took notice at how immensely powerful this young man was. Just what was he capable of?

The cargo doors closed, and they could hear the latching mechanisms loudly bolt the military doors shut. They each took a seat and negotiated the harness type belts. Over the shoulder too, they thought. Could be a rough ride. The engines whined to a pitch beyond the point of comfort. It felt like overtorquing a bolt, like it was about to snap. And then, suddenly the craft lurched off the parking lot and surged into the air. Strange, though. The blades were quiet. It wasn't as loud as they had imagined. The acceleration was remarkable as they climbed 200 feet in what seemed like an instant and reached a speed of more than 100 miles per hour.

They headed for the foothill freeway and then straight down to the El Cajon pass. They were low. Lower than a helicopter is supposed to fly, they thought. Why so low? It was almost as though they were avoiding detection.

"How come we're flying so low?" shouted Rhino.

"We were never here," said Jones, holding his index finger over his lips.

"What's all the secrecy about, Mr. Secret Service man," Bett asked sarcastically.

There was silence for a few moments as Jones looked at Smith. Smith gave a slight nod.

"We're airborne now, ladies and gentlemen. This briefing is top secret and meant for your ears only, Am I clear?" Jones said in an overly loud military command voice.

"Yes sir," said Rhino.

"Whatever GI," said Bett.

"I'm listening," said Dr. Wesson.

Chapter 6

"Drivers, it is time to take your places," said Yuki over her headset to the speaker units in the helmets of all the drivers. "Kramer are you ready?"

"Yes yes. I am ready, Um, just let me know when they start so I can manage the lights. There is not a cop within a mile of the course. Only two are in their cars, the rest are on assignments I have given them in other places." Yuki could manage her race, and Kramer would take care of the traffic and the cops.

He loved this job. He sometimes stuttered when he started to talk, because he had to slow his brain down to make words. Talking was so slow. He would play like cheese to the mice. He would have a prowler here and a loud party there. Nothing threatening or violent. Just enough to get the old *protect and to serve* men in black to be far away so the cats can play. They didn't wear blue. They weren't men in blue any more. They wore black. It was more scary. Like they wanted you to be scared. He was scared. They were so military. He spent a month in lockup when he was 13. The guards were mean, the cops were mean, and the judge was mean. But none of them were as mean as the other inmates.

Dick Daring was his man. He was his best friend. Strong and silent and a pure work of art to watch with a racecar. Who said he couldn't race anymore? Some stupid rule about having two eyes? The patch wasn't so bad. The girls called him Daring Dick, but who knows what that is all about?

"Gentlemen, all wagers are locked in, and the race is about to start," said Yuki with her sparky little smile as her live feed patched into thousands of computers globally. Yuki wasn't her real name. It means chicken in Japanese, but her real name was embarrassing in Japanese. It sounded fine in American, but Makuda means pillow in Japanese. So, she is

22

known worldwide as Yuki. Besides, it makes it impossible for the FBI to track all the earnings and expenditures with fake names in another language.

Six cars would be a full field on the streets of Pasadena. This town had unusually wide streets; very wide, even by wide standards. The Hollywood crowd that founded this area wanted wide streets, and they got them. It was a waste of real estate, but California is nothing if not about wasted space. It made the streets safer than any place in the world. Kids were safe. Parked cars were safe. And racing was safe.

The cars were quiet as they idled into position. It's not like real racing where you want to excite the crowd by revving the engine. This is all about silence until the moment you strike. Nobody knows what's going on until the smoke starts churning from the tires. If you were looking somewhere else, you miss it. That is street racing.

Yuki's little legs flashed her white knee socks in the headlights of the cars as she walked out in front with her signature green scarf. It was neon green, so that is showed up clear and bold on the cameras. She held the scarf in her right hand and reached high over her head. That meant there was three seconds until the start. Some of the cars pushed their throttles, bouncing the engine RPM's against the rev limiter. Two, three, the scarf dropped as if in slow motion, and Yuki dropped to one knee in the middle of the street.

Three cars on her left and three cars on her right, they flashed past her at 60 miles an hour. Yuki was screaming into her microphone to all her fans, "Go!" But no one could hear her. The turbos were sucking all the available air, and the exhaust was drowning out every sound within 500 feet.

Kyle Kramer's program was manipulating traffic lights along the course. Green, green, green for the racers, and red for the crossing streets. Each intersection had team guards on scooters with flashlights to make sure no one turned right on a red light and no pedestrians tried to cross until after the cars had passed. The scooters could ditch a cop better than anything, because they could run the sidewalks in between the apartments and condominiums block after block. Two years, and no team member had ever been apprehended.

The calls began coming in to police dispatch about street racing, but the phone monitors said that the reports were vague and never clear about where exactly they were racing, and well, it seems to have passed. Don't worry about it. The cars jockeyed for position as they went through the gears. With more than a thousand horsepower each, the cars would reach speeds of 150 miles per hour within two blocks. They were dragsters, but there were turns in this course. Just being quick wasn't everything. You also had to be able to drift a corner under power. There was no practice, either. No one knew the place of the race, and there was no way to drive these speeds unless the traffic systems were manipulated. Drag racing, drifting, turning, and sometimes 4 wide around the turns took experience and power and skill. They weren't racing for pink slips. They were racing for cash. Winning $20 thousand in a street race and wowing the online fans, some of them very wealthy, meant new engines, custom transmissions, and exotic lightweight materials could add value to the team. The cars got faster and faster with each passing month.

Within 5 minutes, more than $165 thousand changed hands, and there were a dozen winners. Money would move through a couple of online banking services and arrive in the winning drivers' accounts by morning. The race was over, and all the traffic lights went back to normal operation. All except one.

Chapter 7

Shelly Lasalle was a reporter who wanted to be a news anchor. She was almost there. She had the face and the voice, and she worked her ass off by never missing an assignment. She was a damned good investigative reporter, and after she got her breast implants, she was sure the job would be hers. Then there was that time at the horse track.

The mayor of San Gabriel just happened to be coming out of the main gate after the feature race Shelly was covering as a human interest story on the long tradition of Southern California horse racing. The good mayor was drunk, and as soon as he saw the news camera, he couldn't wait to get in front of it and share his great experience. Shelly should have shut off the camera, but she didn't. She interviewed him with her best smile and her best hair, and the mayor couldn't say a word without slobbering and slurring and looking at her chest. It was live. She was finished. Or so the ABC affiliate told her during her exit interview that evening.

Channel 5 KTLA had mercy on her. Somebody up there was thinking about her, although her inquiries as to whom that might be, proved fruitless. Whoever it was kind of liked the expose' on the mayor. They gave her a news crew in the air instead of sending her to a desk away from the camera. The ladder to the anchor's chair, however, just got a whole lot longer.

She did like her team. She had one of the best camera techs on the West coast, Jimmy James. Her pilot, former captain Rodney "Elvis" Iverson, had flown in three tours in the Middle East and could really negotiate the low-altitude work typical for a news helicopter. When other news crews and police helicopters were in the air, it was just like a battlefield with everyone trying to win the best camera angle when the live action happens. They called him Elvis, not for his hair, but for his legendary karaoke skills. Of course they did the traffic, but they also got to cover the occasional high-speed police chase, a couple of bank robberies, and a multi-car pileup with a fire. Okay, it wasn't sexy, but it paid the bills and at least she was in front of the camera instead of waiting tables.

Today, they were covering the foothill freeway, interstate 210 along the mountains of Pasadena. They could see fairly well through the morning fog that stacked up against the San Gabriel Mountains, but it could be hazardous for drivers on the freeway. California drivers move fast, mostly because they usually drive the newer cars with lots of horsepower and totally unnecessary top speeds. In the fog, those cars fell apart like a daisy smacked with a nine iron when they collided in the fog. It made for great live action news.

"Hey Shelly. I got a strange one for you," said Jimmy. He was connected to the news dispatch, and they had reported a high-speed chase on Colorado Boulevard heading South. "This is a high speed chase, but the lines are all lit up and there is federal chatter in the mix."

"Where is it?" Shelly asked.

"PCC," said Elvis. "I got it dialed in. Hold on. We're turning." He loved this part. Shoving the stick to the right and pulling back on the collector with full throttle to keep the RPM's near 3 thousand 5 hundred could pull about 2 G's in the cabin.

"Jesus, Elvis," Shelly griped. "You know how these turns make me want to puke."

"I love 'em." Said Jimmy.

Elvis kicked the tail up and brought the airspeed up to about 125 knots. "Be there in five minutes," said Elvis. "There it is. Purple Dodge. See it?"

"Yeah yeah, I got it," said Jimmy. "I am zooming so hold it steady."

"It's calm as butter up here this morning."

"Hey, how about a feed here?" Waiting for the red light on the interior cabin camera, she began. "This is Shelly Lasalle live in copter cam channel five near the Pasadena City College. We have been alerted to a high speed chase on

Colorado Boulevard, and we are going to try to bring you that right now."

Jimmy switched to the nose camera that had a perfect fix on the purple Dodge swerving around cars on the Boulevard. "Hey that's weird," said Jimmy over the internal intercom system that was in Shelly's left ear. "All the lights are green in front of that car, and all the lights behind it are red. The cop cars are getting fouled in the cross traffic, and the Dodge is pulling away in clear traffic. It's headed for the Foothill."

"We're coming in behind them," said Elvis. "I got him. Opening up the twin fifties. Oh, sorry. Wrong helicopter." He smiled. Combat was much more fun when you could shoot what you saw.

"How fast are we going, Elvis?" Shelly asked over the live TV feed, as the purple Dodge was not switched to full screen.

"We're clocking him at 100 on the Boulevard. No one is even close to him except us. The police helicopter is a 6-cylinder Bell with a top speed of 90 knots. They're done."

"Stay on him," she said on the intercom. "Channel five viewers, this purple Dodge, I believe it is a Challenger, has outrun all the police cars and the police helicopter. Our jet ranger news helicopter has a top speed of 165, so we will stay with him and keep you informed."

"He's slowing down. Hold on. He's getting on the freeway heading South. Hang on, I am going in lower."

"Elvis, are you hearing this feed from dispatch?" Jimmy asked. "They're saying maintain 2 thousand feet."

"That's bull shit. They don't want a clear picture through this light fog. We're almost out of it, and I can get you a good view of this guy's plate from 500 feet," Elvis complained.

"I'm just saying dispatch is ordering 2 thousand feet."

"Go for it, Elvis," said Shelly. "We can break this story with a plate."

"What the hell?" said Elvis. "I'm firewalled and on a glide slope doing 170 knots. He's pulling away."

"What?" Shelly switched again to the live feed audio. "Channel five viewers, our news helicopter is traveling at its fastest rated speed of 175 knots, and this purple Dodge is pulling away from us heading South on the Foothill Freeway. I have never seen a car this fast."

"Holy smokes. Hang on, we doing evasive," said Elvis as he pulled back on the stick to climb to a higher altitude.

"Oh my God," grunted Shelly over the intercom as she sunk down in her jump seat. "What the hell are you doing?"

"We got company, and it ain't local," said Elvis.

"What the hell is that?" shouted Jimmy.

"That, sports fans is something very dark and very fast."

"I see that it is black," said Shelly. "But what is it?"

"I mean it's dark. No radar signature. It is a stealth craft. Top government stuff. Somebody very important is heading along this freeway in the same direction as that purple Dodge, only a whole lot faster. They're clocking over 190."

"What? Say again dispatch," shouted Jimmy into his mike. "Well, shit."

"Get that helicopter on camera, Jimmy," shouted Shelly.

"I can't. That's what they were saying to me. Don't shoot the helicopter. Let it go."

"That is so much bull shit, Jimmy. Turn off the station feed and get me some footage of that helicopter. I wanna know what the hell that thing is doing in our neighborhood, and what it has to do with that Dodge." She slammed her butt down in the jump seat like she was throwing a fit.

"Hang on. I'm doing a loop with the feed. Got it. I have a 10 second window. I got a secret," he said to himself over the intercom. He centered the black helicopter and began filming. It was just in front and below them at perhaps 300 feet off the deck. The camera auto locked on the target and followed it while zooming with digital perfection. "You might be invisible to radar, but I see you. Three, two one, I'm out. I have to go back to the live feed. Inside. Inside"

"This is Shelly Lasalle like in the traffic Live at Five helicopter over the Foothill Freeway where a high speed chase has resulted in the purple Dodge getting away. That car is out of our range and too fast for our equipment. We are returning to the Pasadena area to show you the live action from the snarl of traffic in the aftermath. Back to you, central command."

"We're out," said Jimmy.

"Hey guys?" asked Elvis.

"What now, a flying saucer?" asked Shelly.

"You wish. I think I know where they're going."

"Where?" they both said at the same time.

"Victorville. There is an old test strip there. I used to fly acrobatics out of there."

"That's over an hour away," said Jimmy.

"Not if we go over the mountains. We can be there in 30 minutes."

"Do we have the gas?" asked Shelly.

"Oh yeah," said Elvis.

"It's on the way to Pasadena, isn't it?" she asked.

"Sure it is," said Elvis.

"Well, something sure as shit doesn't make any sense here. My nose says we need to do some investigation. What do you say, guys?"

"I'm in," said Jimmy.

"Hang on," said Elvis. "We need some altitude to do this. I can catch a tail wind at 10 thousand feet. Hey guys? This cabin is not pressurized, and we will be just below the ceiling for oxygen, so you should relax and stay in your seat. Okay?"

Chapter 8

"Kramer, do you have the program done?" asked Dick. This was a great car. The winnings from the last two races allowed him to turbocharge this Dodge Challenger. It was tricky, because the motor was relatively high compression, and he didn't want to blow the heads off it. The supercharged version was okay, but he knew with the turbo he could get over a thousand horsepower out of it on the top end, where it was needed most.

"Yep. I had some code to write this morning, but it is good to go. And, I added the nitrous." Kramer was a prodigy at computer technology, but he also understood chemistry and mechanical engineering. He was self taught, but as he always said, "Professors are obsolete the moment they got out of school, and they've been out of school a long time." Besides, he knew why they liked teaching. They liked being the smartest person in the room. "But, what if they weren't the smartest anymore?"

Kyle Kramer had ADHD in the worst way. He was a poster child for the disorder, but his mom was a drug addict. She had no money and didn't care about Kyle when he was young. He never got drugged down to match the other kids in class. Instead, he claimed he bottled it up and fed it back into his brain. He learned to focus on many things at once like spinning plates on the end of long flexible rods. He would spin one plate, and then go to another and another, until he had them all spinning all the time.

Then, he started seeing patterns between the disciplines. He called them transitory relationships. Chemistry became poetry. C++ became metallurgy and crystallography. The magnetic fields around gaseous molecules became like flowers that could be germinated with other magnetic fields. All of these different sciences became artistic parts of one another, and Kyle became the master painter.

"It will pack more oxygen into the "P" orbitals."

"Kyle. I don't think gasses have "P" orbitals. Now come on."

"Well, no they don't. But adding the magnets to the container and the stainless steel fuel lines allows us to create virtual "P" orbitals. More oxygen. Changes the stoichiometry."

"Hey, that makes me hungry. You want some IHOP?"

"Yeah. I like pancakes."

Just then there was a loud knock on the steel rollup door. "Police. Open the door!"

"Oh no. No way. Dick, I can't go to jail. No, no." Kramer was prone to panic. It wasn't an ordinary panic that you can reason with. You have to occupy Kyle's brain when he is faced with a situation.

"Kyle, get in the car and hook up the laptop. Put your harness on."

There was a trust that calmed him when Dick spoke like this. He knew there was a plan, and Dick was his favorite person. He was like a brother and his best friend. He never panicked. He always knew what to do.

Dick slid into his cockpit seat and strapped himself in. "Access the traffic system and set us up for a clean run to the freeway South."

"The airstrip?"

"Yeah."

"Shit. Shit. Shit. "

"What is it now, forgot to charge your laptop?"

"It's my fault. I see what happened now. I missed a light last night. It stayed green all night, and their TMS guy found my hack."

31

"Well, I suppose those guys out there are not here to collect for the policeman's ball," said Dick.

"If you don't open this door, we will be forced to cut it open and add the charge of resisting arrest." They were elevating the energy now. Pasadena cops liked to do that. Most of them were former military guys who would work for a cop's pay as long as they got to keep eating steroids and got to bust some heads now and then. Street racers were a public enemy. Hackers were terrorists. And street racer hackers were nothing short of a federal trophy for a local cop.

"We gotta go, and we gotta go now," said Dick.
"I'm in, I'm in. I have the fuel management system and the traffic system. Should I open the door?" Kyle was calming now. He was focused on the problem and the formulas were churning in his head like polyurethane foam.

"I'm opening the door. Gentlemen, start your engines."
"Here we go." Dick flipped the switches to apply power to the ignition and fuel management computers. The light went green, and he flipped the switch for the electric fuel pumps and pressed the button to start the motor. It thumped against the frame and rumbled to life. "Full tanks. Let's roll"

The door was barely open four feet, not enough for the cops to bend down and start entering their shop, but far enough that the Dodge was heading for the opening. It would be close. The car went sideways a little as the rear wheels spun on the shiny epoxy floors, but Dick corrected for it. The car surged forward toward the rollup door.

"Stop the car! Stop the car!" shouted the policeman who ducked his head under the still opening door. He went for his gun. Dick shot him the bird with his hand out the window and he sliced past him into the parking lot. There were a dozen cars and a police helicopter waiting in the parking lot.

"Kyle, help me out here," Dick whined.

"Go left. Go left, Over the grass and onto Colorado. I got your lights."

"Here we go." Dick pressed the throttle and the turbos started to spin. The Challenger lurched over the curb and onto the grass before spinning tires over the sidewalk and onto the asphalt. He drove between an SUV and a cruiser, and was pointed in the right direction. The police helicopter was directly overhead. They had a long way to go past the city college and Cal Tech and then left to the on-ramp. The wheel flipped back and forth as Dick negotiated the police cars in front of him.

"Don't hit anything. The intercooler is packed in the front behind the fenders," Kyle squeaked.

"I got it. I got it. One more. Here we go." The car was running like a dream, but now was the test. He had never raced this car. What would it do when it got going fast?

"That's a gas powered copter. Can you do something?"

"Working on it. I can hack the governor. I can limit his top speed."

"Do it, we're running." The traffic lights were all green ahead of them, and not a car was on the road. It was strange, Dick thought for a moment. Colorado Boulevard with no cars on it. In the daytime. Really strange moment. He mashed the throttle all the way to the floor. The motor came to life as the RPM's climbed. The transmission shifted to keep the engine below the rev limiter, and they were doing 120 by the time 6 seconds focused on them.

"Turn 'em off, turn the green lights off."

" They're all on automatic now," said Kyle. One by one the lights turned red behind them, which meant the cross traffic could proceed across and onto the busiest boulevard in Pasadena. Within a few seconds, what promised to be a high speed chase, turned into a swift Sunday tour through the Pasadena shopping district.

"Coming up on PCC and Cal tech. Get ready to drift onto San Gabriel and hit the main on ramp. It's two lanes wide," said Kyle.

"That helicopter caught up when I slowed down to make this turn. He is right over us. Can you do something about him?"

"Wait until you get on the freeway. You'll see."

They both held their breath as the car slid all four tires sideways drifting left onto San Gabriel Boulevard. The car powered through the turn, but not light and nimble like the Honda. The car got close to the curb, but it soon straightened out. Dick knew how to drive this car. The on ramp came up quickly, and the helicopter was low, right on top of them. It looked like it was going to land in front of them.

Dick darted left and then right toward the on ramp, slipping under the rails of the helicopter. Dick floored the car. This time the turbos whistled loudly.

"Get ready," said Kyle. "Three, two one." Kyle pressed the F8 key and the magnetized nitrous poured into the plenum just behind the turbos. It swirled and compressed to three atmospheres and pounded through the intake valves to mix with direct injection in the cylinders. The purple Dodge Challenger blasted to a speed of 180 miles an hour within a few seconds, leaving the police helicopter at the altar.

"God, I love American muscle," said Dick as he gripped wheel to keep the car pointed straight.

Chapter 9

Robert Riker was an engineer. He got married in his sophomore year at Tennessee Technological University to his high school sweetheart. They were going to wait until he graduated, but they found out she was not able to have children. That was the only reason they were waiting. He always said that you shouldn't get married until you were ready to start your empire. You know, start having kids. Without the possibility of children, they decided they were meant to be together, so they set a date and got married in the Smoky Mountains.

He graduated with honors and had some very rewarding positions in the automobile manufacturing industry. They moved quite a few times, and each time it meant more money and bigger challenges. After 20 years in the industry, and never being apart a single day, they found out why she couldn't have children. It was mysterious, really. That cancer could hide for so long, and then suddenly come out of hiding and take a life that quickly.

The doctors said that chemo wouldn't save her. In fact, it would make her final months even worse, make her lose her hair, and take her down even faster. She loved her hair, and she loved being Mrs. Robert Riker. She would always be with him. There was a link between them they could not explain. Like they were together before this world, or something. They knew it.

He decided to take up his second passion; politics. The whole process of the presidential election drove the engineer side of him crazy. So much money. $5 million just to get on the ballot. TV, radio, printed ads, and all the action committees that wanted to buy a piece of the candidate for later, in case they needed something passed or blocked in Congress. It was so corrupt.

And the candidates seemed to beat one another up so badly before the election, and then after the election they would be seen golfing together, or sailing together. To him, it seemed like everyone was in the same Party. They just faked it in front of the public, so they would think they had a choice between two different ideologies. "Why couldn't anyone else see that?" he would ask himself.

Then, one day he had a crazy idea. Really, it was quite insane. Each election there were about 500 presidential candidates. Almost all of them had problems getting enough signatures to get on the ballots in every State. They didn't have the cash to pay the State election commissions to get on the ballot. They could buy a TV slot or make it into the debates. What would happen if a candidate put his entire platform on YouTube and Snapchat and debated each national candidate in the virtual world? He was an engineer, after all. He could do that. All people would have to do is write his name on the ballot and vote for him.

It was like an election made for this type of approach. The Republican candidate was just as detestable as the Democrat. They argued with each other like academics, citing legislation they had backed or not backed. They jockeyed for hours in national debates over points of law, immigration policy and over which one would keep the country safe against terrorism. It made everyone sick of the election.

So, what did he have to lose? He began taking on the issues one by one and crafting his speeches. Each YouTube was kept to less than 10 minutes and straight to the point. Within 6 months, his channel had more than 200 thousand subscribers. That was not nearly enough, he thought. What he did not know, was that there were thousands upon thousands of viral connections to each one of those YouTube files. He was only seeing the ones that connected to his channel. The rest were connected to the links on other people's social media pages. It turned into tens of millions, and then hundreds of millions. The only thing missing was the main stream media taking notice. To them, Robert Riker had zero chance of being elected. No one was going to write in a name for president. Never happen.

The night of the final presidential debate between the two nominees was surreal. The CNN anchor asked a question about ethics in politics. The republican candidate pointed his finger at the Democrat, and it was like someone had dropped two fighting cocks into the ring. They each stepped away from their Plexiglas podiums and got inches away from punches. The anchor left his desk and tried to separate them, fearing that their integrity was on the line, and then it got worse.

The live program did not have a delay on the feed. The profanity got so bad, so quickly, that the director had to break away to a commercial. It was too late. The hair was messed up. The reputations were soiled. The audience was disgusted. They had to do something. So they did. It was a landslide. Robert Riker was elected as president with an unprecedented write-in election campaign.

Millions of young people and millions of middle-aged people, and millions of web-savvy seniors wrote in his name. He won.

When he took the oath, it was like he had stepped into another world. The next 100 hours of his life seemed like non-stop briefings and meetings, and forms to sign. He shook so many hands, his right hand was swollen. Still, he didn't feel welcome. It was like going to a massive Bingo night for the first time and winning the grand prize. Everyone was happy for you, but at the same time raging inside because you were nobody, and you had not played as many cards as they had. You had not paid your dues. You weren't even supposed to be here.

The Secret Service agents sort of became his guides. He trusted them. Sure, they were there to take a bullet for him, but there was more to it than that. He felt they wouldn't steer him wrong. He could ask them anything, just about. The chief of staff was the same as with the last president. She knew all the protocols and the importance of meetings and briefings and which reporters to trust to write the right things. She knew secrets, too. Too many.

Sitting here on the edge of this strange bed, alone, again thinking about the path of his life and how it had led him to this place and this time made him feel lost. For the first time in his life, he could not see what to do next. Maybe he was in over his head. Maybe this was not such a good idea. His vice president was the former speaker of the House and a good man. Maybe he could take it from here.

He got up to get a drink from the cold glass bottle of Perrier that was still sitting in the silver ice bucket on the table across the enormous bedroom of the White House. There were little lights along the wainscot walls of the bedroom. They kept the floor fairly well lit to nighttime eyes. I guess they didn't want the president to stub his toe or something during the night. Looking down, it was easy to walk around the early American furniture and the floor lamp to reach the table. Perrier kind of cut the crud in the throat, he felt. It was kind of crisp and refreshing, and after a small burp it calmed the stomach. Got rid of the butterflies that seemed to be there all the time now. Like falling backward in a chair, he felt he had to catch himself every moment of the day.

The fizzy water was great as he took a few gulps from the green glass bottle. He spun the lid back in place to keep it from going flat and dropped into back into the ice water in the bucket. He noticed the time on the out of place digital clock; 3:00 AM. Turning toward the bed he knew he needed, but did not want, he froze. Standing next to his bed was a tall, dark-suited figure.

"Mr. President?" asked the figure.
"It's okay. I was just getting a drink of water. I'm okay," recognizing it was a secret service agent. He had not seen this man before, but then it was usually the day shift team that ushered him around.
"I am agent Yafil Al Hadid," said the olive skinned man. He was amazingly crisp and his suit seemed to fit perfectly. He was not truly built like a normal agent. He was quite tall, perhaps six feet five inches, but he was more athletic looking that most. Normally, they looked like they had two inches of armor under their shirts, but you knew it was muscle just waiting to spring into action. Former military guys with perfect records going back to birth, it seemed.

"Would you come with me, Mr. President?" he asked so smoothly it massaged the ear.
"What, now? I'm in my pajamas," said Riker.
"We only have a few minutes, Mr. President. There has been an event. It is important you come with me now. Downstairs."
"We're on the ground floor, agent..uh. What was your name again?"
"Yafil Al Hadid. It roughly translates to *the iron bar.*"
"Okay, Iron bar. What do you mean downstairs?"
"Please, Mr. President," he said extending his outstretched hand to him as though to lead him in the night.
"My slippers. Hold on," he said as he walked toward the bed and slipped on his leather slippers. They were more like moccasins. He walked to the White House kitchen one night barefooted to make a sandwich. The marble floors were cold, but the next morning the housekeepers were upset about it. His bare feet had left prints on the glossy finish from the bedroom all the way to the kitchen and back. The next time he wore his moccasins and never heard a word about it.

He instinctively turned right out of the bedroom to go down the hall, but the agent stopped him and they turned left instead. "That's a dead end," he said.

Holding his finger up to his lips to be quiet, he silently walked down to the last wainscot panel and held a pass card up to the mahogany panel in the corner. There was a quiet thump, and the wall hinged open to reveal another hallway sloping downward. They passed behind the wall, and Hadid pulled the bar on the back of the door wall and latched it shut. It was locked from the inside now.

They walked down to the right in a spiral for about 30 feet and came to a steel door. Again, the magnetic pass card was used, and the door slid open, revealing an elevator capable of holding perhaps ten people. It was about 12 feet deep and 4 feet wide. They entered the elevator, and the steel door slid silently shut. The card was applied again, this time with several numbers punched into a keypad on the elevator wall, along with Hadid's thumb print on the square pad next to the number pad.

Wow, he thought. Now that is biometric security. The elevator dropped quickly for about 20 seconds and stopped. The steel door opened and revealed a large room. They exited the elevator and the steel door closed behind them.

"Follow me, Mr. President," Hadid spoke normally now. His accent was middle eastern, but it was amazingly smooth. It was not guttural like the Saudis or harsh like Persian. It was ancient sounding. He opened the next door by placing his hand on a blue pad at the top of a pedestal about 8 feet in front of the door and to the right. The door buzzed, and they stepped forward to push it open.

The next room was plush and comfortable looking. The chairs were leather, and the walls were paneled with cherry and had brass sconces near the ten foot ceiling that offered a kind of celestial lighting that left the room warm and manly. Hadid motioned for Riker to sit down. He did. Hadid walked through the hallway opening and returned with a small tray with coffee and some cups. Behind him walked two other men, dressed as agents as well, very white and very tall. Four men deep under the White House with coffee at 3 AM.

"Mr. President, thank you for coming," said the tallest of the white figures in dark agent-like suits. His voice was deep, and there was no accent at all.

"Like I had a choice. What's going on?" asked Riker.

"Mr. President, what you are about to hear may not come easy, but it is vital that you listen and open your mind to the possibilities," said the second white figure, also with no accent but with a much higher, almost sweet sounding voice. His diction was perfect, like a computer sound almost.

"We are all secret service, but we are a special department inside this service. Our allegiance goes back more than 6 thousand years when the original merging occurred. We call it the union of the polarity. Each generation has been given this story to keep safe. It is an oral tradition, often speculated by ancient civilizations in pictures and glyphs, but never written down. We were waiting for a prophesied leader to come. You are that leader, Mr. President." Hadid was solid and smooth and the words rolled off his tongue like gold. He was transfixed. He felt a little shiver down his spine. He took a sip of the coffee Hadid had poured while he as he talking. All was flawless. Like a ritual that was rehearsed in its perfection. He was reminded of the tea pouring ceremony the Japanese ambassador had demonstrated in his most recent visit to the White House. The placement of the cup, the holding of the porcelain pot with the left hand gently touching the lid so that it did not rattle or fall off while pouring. The coffee was brought to exactly the same level in all four cups with care and forethought. The hands were steady and smooth like no machine could ever do. Like leading a dance or a song, it was painted in the air and set back in place without a sound.

"Guys, uh agents. I am lost here. I am in my pajamas, and I don't know what's going on. Help me out here," said Riker as he realized something very important was about to happen.

The agent with the high voice spoke first, "My name is John, Mr. President. Last night in the Gulf of Mexico there was an event that indicated to us that the grand separation is about to occur."
"The grand what?"
"It is an event that is prophesied to occur as the two Earths come apart," said John.
"Two Earths? Okay, guys. I have to admit this sounds a little too much like science fiction. What happened? In the Gulf, what happened?"

"At 21:35, gravitational waves induced a reverse Tsunami in the Gulf of Mexico. It was reported by observers on watch at Deepwater Horizon, one of the most modern oil rigs in the Gulf region. The rig was nearly destroyed and caused a spill that ignited and is burning out of control on the sea surface as we speak. Equipment is being moved into place, and the story is being crafted at the Department of the Interior," explained John.

"So what is so strange about that? Why drag me down here in my PJ's to tell me this?" He was getting frustrated now. The engineer in him wanted someone to state the problem.

"It was prophesied, Mr. President," said the taller white agent.
"I'm sorry. What was your name?"
"Apologies. Enoch is my name, Mr. President."

"How about Bob? You guys can call me Bob while we're down here. Okay? Okay?"

"Yes sir," said Hadid.

"Oh geeze. Forget it. Just tell me about this prophesy."

"The End times," John paused, "Bob. There are two planets that merged during the Great Flood. In the end times, they begin to go out of phase. Great cataclysms are predicted as they come apart. They are made of two different energies, higher and lower. Like us. Like our bodies. We are not sure of the exact details, but there is someone who knows this very well. She is a professor."

Enoch interrupted, "Not a professor. She is an associate professor at Cal Tech. Her thesis is correct, but we need the details in her study to know exactly when it will occur."

"I see. Well, how do we get this associate professor, uh, I'm sorry do you have a name?"

"Dr. Loretta Wesson, Mr., uh Bob," said Hadid.

"Make it happen. When can she be here?"

"We are sending two agents there as we speak. It will take them 5 hours to reach her," said Hadid.

"Who else knows about this?"

"That is complicated, Mr. President," John winced as he said the words, but he was trained to be comfortable with saying it. There is another ancient order as old as ours. They also know, but they are in control of the world."

"The world? I don't think so. This is the USA," said Riker.

"That's what I mean, Mr. President. It's complicated. Since 1910, this order also has controlled the money system of America as well. The two men you beat in the election both are part of this syndicate. You are outside this network. You also are part of the prophecy. We know it, and they know it. They will be coming for you, now that the signs have begun."

"Why now? What difference does it make if we're all going to die anyway?"

"We are not going to die, Mr. President," said John. "We are alive now on the Earth, but we do not die."

"It is a war, Mr. President," Hadid was more comfortable with saying it as well. There is a dark leader on the Earth who leads the choice. He is winning the war, and this is why we are here. You. Us. It is why we are here."

"When you say 'war' I get the feeling you don't mean with missiles and bombs, right?"

"We need the professor's work. It will be easier to explain," said John.

"We have much to do before then. We must be at the remote command post by dawn tomorrow," said Hadid as he rose to gather the tray with the coffee and go to the other room.

"One more thing. Why all the secrecy? I get it that we're in a hurry, but we're 200 feet under the White House."

"It is vital that at least one of us is by your side at all times now, Mr. President. There are others that…they will try to kill you now," and with that, Enoch moved to the door and motioned for John to escort the president to the elevator. "Let's go now."

Chapter 10

"Whiskey Bravo two six niner?"

"Whiskey Bravo two six niner, go ahead."

"Please advise fueling status and team status."

"We are fueled, canopies open, and awaiting flight plan, tower."

"Lieutenant, we are confirming sortie at this time. Orders will be forthcoming at pattern exit. Stand by for launch codes."

"Say again, tower. Did you say launch codes?

"Stand by. Switch to channel three zero." Lieutenant Jasper switched his radio selector to three zero. That meant the message was encrypted. There were Ham folks around that had picked up their chatter before and published in the Victorville Tribune. But if command was giving launch codes, that meant their ordinance would be live. Maybe this wasn't a drill, but how could that be. They were in freaking Victorville watching a flock of aging SR-71 blackbirds.

"Three zero roger."

"Launch codes are being uploaded. This is not a drill. Your flight plan will be provided once you are out of pattern."

It must not be much. Normally, they would get a flight plan in an envelope and go as a team into the ready room and rehearse it down to the last drop of fuel. Climb outs, strafing runs with the 30mm cannon and drops of ordinance. The A-10 isn't a fighter jet, and doesn't go very fast compared to other military jets, but it is a fearful sound for targets on the ground. The gun was so large it ran all the way under the pilot's seat and into the rear fuselage. It was a flying gun that could rip a tank to shreds or turn a building into dust.

This plan was different. Something quick. Something close by. Something very, very secret.

"Roger launch codes are received."

Chapter 11

"I-15 is coming up. We're going east, remember," said Kyle as he glanced up from his laptop. They were still going about 180 miles an hour, but the Foothill Freeway, I-210, was one of the smoothest stretches of road in Southern California.

"Okay. Shut the nitrous off, I'm letting off to make this turn," said Dick as he flexed his hands from gripping the steering wheel for the last 20 minutes.

"Nitrous off. Exhaust temperatures are around 850. Pretty good. I'm happy," said Kyle.

"I think I can make this turn at 100," the tires were hot and able to grip the road with only a slight sound of breaking loose as the two-lane interchange was negotiated.

"It's all uphill from here, so watch your exhaust temperatures," said Kyle.

"I think it can take 12 hundred."

"Not for very long. The blades are aluminum."

"Relax, I'll keep under 150."

"I'm just saying we don't want to melt anything."

"How are you feeling Kyle?"

"I'm good. I'm good. I'm hungry."

"We still have some slim Jim's at the shed, right?"

"Screw a bunch of slim Jim's. I want a burger or something."

"You'll last. My mom's old Riviera is at the shed. We'll go to V'ville for supper. What do you say?"

"Yeah, I'm down. I hope they don't have a statewide warrant for us."

"Yeah, well the gubment has bigger fish to fry, I'm hoping. Hey, that reminds me, see if our deposit from last night is in the bank yet."

"Hold on. Crap. No network here. We're in the boonies. Hold on, I will use the cell."

"While you're looking, I just wanted to say thank you. You did a great job back there."

"I nearly got us busted. I can't believe I left that light latched. Um. Yes. It's in. Nice. $55,450. That will help us finish the fuel project."

"Or by a new truck. We need a truck."

"Oh come on. That coupled nitrous is almost a fuel by itself. I have two tanks left."

"Oh yeah. Where are those tanks, by the way?" asked Dick.

"Right where we left them. In the shed next to the filter."

"Cool."

Chapter 12

"We're ten minutes out, sir."

Smith reached forward to touch Bett's knee. Her eyes opened. She had dozed off during the 30-minute flight from Pasadena to Victorville. The airstrip was in sight and the helicopter was diving along the east side of the San Bernardino mountains to stay on the deck. The pilot was flying, rather than using the ALS, because of the passengers. At that speed, passengers would be screaming if the ALS was controlling the altitude. He could make it smoother and still stay below Edwards Air Force Base radar.

"It's time to get ready to transfer to the jet. We're heading for Camp David," said Smith.

"Are going to see the president there?" asked Loretta.

"You have been requested to be there and ready to explain your thesis.

"My thesis? You mean on planetary core structure?"

"Actually, it is the part you left out of the thesis they are most interested in," said Jones.

"Why?" She got a look on her face like someone had just seen through her hidden thesis inside her published version. "Has there been an event?"

Smith and Jones looked at each other for a moment. "Let's just say you were the only geologist whose theory accommodated empirical data," said Jones.

"Empirical data? What empirical data? Jesus, will somebody please let me know what it going on?"

"That's all we are authorized to say. We're not there yet," said Smith.

"Sir, we have a minor problem," said the pilot over the intercom.

Smith leaned forward to the pilot's seat to look out the front glass. Down below on the strip was the white G-7 government jet sitting right where they had left it. Next to the jet was parked a purple Dodge challenger.

Chapter 13

"Oh, I'm glad we're here. My butt is numb," said Kyle. As they came around the gate to the abandoned air strip where they tested their fastest ideas far from the prying eyes of other street racers, they both were shocked. There, sitting in dazzling glory was a brand new G-7 private jet.

"That is really bigger than I thought one would be," said Dick. "That's a what kind of plane?"

"That is a G-7. Very expensive. Those winglets and the extra center tank means it's a trans-con version."

"Trans-con?"

"Able to go across the pond. Long range version. Maybe 8,000 miles."

Dick whistled. "How much does one of those run?"

"Hmm. Depends on the electronics, but at least $10 million."

"Okaaay. So, tell me why a $10 million jet is sitting on our runway with nobody around?

Kyle laughed as he unbuckled his harness and opened the passenger door. He slid his laptop onto the seat and stepped onto the tarmac. It was cracked concrete, but relatively smooth. The whole place looked like a scene out of Duke Nuke 'em, but they had made good use of the old abandoned air strip with an 11 thousand foot runway. "Isn't possession nine tenths of the law?"

"Yeah, nice try your honor. I think that little wreath on the door might say something." Dick leaped out and ran over to where the air stairs would come down. "Um. I make this to be United States Secret Service." He started to back away in a slight state of panic. He started to look around for a sniper somewhere. "Hey Kyle? What is that?"

"What is what?"

"That." Dick pointed to the North at the small black craft coming straight for them about 100 feet off the ground like a bat out of hell.

"Um. Shit. I don't know. Shit. Okay, that is a Black Hawk attack helicopter. Run!"

They both ran for the short tower room. This airstrip never had an active tower. It was for test pilots and training during the Korean War and was used during the Vietnam Era. It was faded white concrete to keep the brutal desert sun from roasting the people inside. Once the sun hit the mountains in the late afternoon, it was quite nice. The upper desert would cool down to a comfortable and dry 80 degrees, even in the summer.

As they reached the door, the black craft was on them. It was so fast and so quiet and never fired a shot. It quickly landed, and two men in suits came running out and toward the building. "United States Secret Service," shouted Smith. "Show your hands and come out slowly."

Kyle and Dick emerged from the old building like they had been caught trespassing on an abandoned amusement park. "Hey guys. Nice jet," said Dick.

"Who are you?" asked Jones holding his jacket open so he could reach his firearm.

"Hey hey. I'm Richard Daring and this is my partner in crime, Kyle Kramer," said Dick. "Hah, I said crime, I mean he is my, technician. He's an engineer. Sort of."

"Richard Daring. Dick Daring?" asked Bett running up behind the two agents. "The race car driver?"

"Yeah, that would be me. Why?"

"Guys, this is Dick Daring. He's world famous. Well, he was," said Bett. She was jealous, sort of. She always wanted to drive race cars, but settled for riding Harley's instead. Judging from the scar and patch over Dick's right eye, she had made the right decision; so far.

"What are you doing here?" Asked Smith.

"What are we doing here? What are you doing here," squeaked Kyle. He had been silent on the edge panic up to this point. "This is our airstrip. Well, we use it to test cars, for a long time now. You're trespassing," he said pointing his freckled finger at Smith from twenty feet away.

"So we are," said Smith. "So we are. We actually need to be leaving now, so we would appreciate it if you didn't know we were here."

"Ah. Where?" said Dick. "I didn't see anything. Did you see anything, Kyle?"

"Me? Nope."

"Rhino? Put the boxes in the tail cargo area please," said Jones without turning around. He still didn't trust these two. He did look at the car though. "Nice car."

"Thanks," they both said at once.

"Sir, we need 10 minutes to preflight," said the pilot of the helicopter who was now preparing to fly the jet.

"You have 5," said Smith. The two uniformed men turned with their clipboards and began checking the plane. One opened the door and dropped the air stairs. He slipped up the stairs and into the plane. "What are you guys doing out here?"

"Well, we sort of had to get out of town fast, and we use this strip to test cars. We have a lab and some equipment here, back here in this bungalow," said Dick.

"What kind of lab?" asked Jones. He was curious. These two looked like grease monkeys, but they didn't sound like one.

"We experiment with magnetically aligned nitrous oxide for enhance fuel systems," blurted out Kyle while looking around at Dick. He hoped he wasn't giving anything away, but it was the secret service, and they did ask.

The co-pilot emerged from the cabin slightly. "Sir, we have a problem."

"Report, please," ordered Smith.

"There is chatter from Edwards. They're scrambling two A-10's. Sir, they have launch codes."

"Rhino! Are those boxes aboard?" yelled Jones.

"Yes sirs," said Rhino.

"A-10's? Hold on. Hold on. Hold on," stuttered Kyle. He ran for the Dodge and retrieved his laptop. "Hey hey, I'm still up. Gimme a second." His hands flew over the keyboard and in a few seconds he yelled out. "I got 'em."

"You got what? Remember we talked about specifics?" said Dick.

"A-10's. They're old. I hacked one once. I can hack their flight deck," said Kyle.

"Sir, we have to go low and fast to stay under radar, but we have to fly right over Edwards for the shortest route," said the pilot as he walked up with his electronic clipboard.

"What about going over them?" asked Smith.

"Our ceiling is 55 thousand in this jet. Edwards controls all the way up"

"Up to where?"

"Well, all the way, sir."

"Why can't you go higher?" asked Bett.

"Oxygen. There' no oxygen. Engines flame out," spouted Kyle.

"Basically, that's right," said the pilot.

"I can fix that. I can make this work," said Kyle as he began typing on his laptop again. "Dick, the engines are GE, right?

"Lemme check," said Dick running to the front of the port engine. "Yes. General Electric, it says here."

"I can do this. We have the stuff. Can you fit two bottles in the cargo hold?"

"There's plenty of room in there," said Rhino.

"Come on. Come with me," said Dick.

The group ran to the Bungalow about 50 yards away. Dick spun the combination and opened the rollup door. There were about 20 bottles of various types of compressed gas. "These two. Get these two. Careful. They're heavy," said Dick. "Here's a dolly."

Rhino grabbed the dolly and began wheeling the two bottles toward the jet's ready cargo hold.

"What size jets?" Dick shouted out the door at Kyle.

"No jets! Grab the three-eighths lines," squeaked Kyle. "And get the drill"

Dick grabbed the coils of three-eighths inch stainless steel lines and the proper compression unions and solenoids to make up the injection system. He was mapping the system in his mind, but the bulk of the work had to be done inside Kramer's crazy brain. Too little, and the engine floods and flames out. Too much and they turn into a pretty firework in the sky.

"We're going to need a battery too. The jet runs on a 24-volt system," said Kyle.

"Hey, Bett. Grab that deep cycle battery over there." He didn't know why he asked her to get the battery. Something just told him by looking at her that she wouldn't say no. She didn't. They all headed for the jet. "Grab a ladder, will ya?" Dick pointed to Jones.

Within twenty minutes, they had the bottles jammed into the back of the jet along with the battery for the solenoids and a spool of wire to make the connection inside the cabin. Dick drilled a hole through the side of the outer skin and routed the stainless steel line through the hole. The pipes fed directly through the side of the engine cases just behind the compressor of each motor.

Kyle was still jamming away on the laptop, which he had now transferred to a swivel seat in the cabin of the G-7. "Hey guys? We have an update," yelled Kyle. "I am into the flight deck of the A-10's. They have no orders."

"What?" asked Smith.

"They have no orders. They are climbing out and that is the end of the string, but they have launch codes for two Hellfire missiles each."

54

"Hellfires? Damn. They plan on catching us on the ground. This is standard tactical protocol. No orders until you're airborne. We have to leave, people," said Smith.

"What do you mean, people?" We're not going," said Dick pointing back and forth to Kyle and him.

"If you don't go, you die. Understand?"

"Why? What did we do?"

"You saw. You die. You go with us, you have a chance of living" said Smith.

"Well, since you put it like that, I guess we're going with you. Hand me that line wrench will you?"

"Guys, they're rolling. Canopies up," said Kyle.

"Sir, we have completed our preflight. We're ready," said the pilot to Smith. Turning to recheck the cargo area, Dick and Rhino came crawling out. Noticing the stainless steel line coming out of a neat hole in the outside skin and going into the engine casing, the pilot shouted, "What the hell did you just do?" Facing Smith, he said, "Sir I have no idea how this will affect the aircraft."

"Don't you worry about it, Cap," said Dick. "Everything is under control."

"Oh yeah? Who's control?"

"His," said Dick pointing to Kyle chewing on a pencil while flying over the keyboard of his laptop.

"Okay, let's go," said Smith. They bounded up the air stairs and hauled in and secured the door. "Spool up, men. We're wheels up in one minute."

"Sir, I do not have the flight plan into the computer yet. We'll have to do it once we're airborne," said the co-pilot. "There's weather or something. I cannot get a clean arrival time, no matter what I do."

"Okay. We'll do it in the air. Take off and head East," said Smith.

"East? We can't go east, that will put us on an intercept with Edwards," said the pilot.

"Sit down and belt in, people. We're rolling," ordered Smith.

The engines began spooling up and the jet rolled forward to taxi to the South end of the runway. There would be no clearance needed. This was truly visual flight rating, fly by the seat of your pants, combat style flying until they got out of range of the A-10's. Still, the G-7 had to roll nearly a mile to the South to be able to take off, and there was plenty of foreign material like sticks and tumbleweeds along the way, so the engines had to be kept at a low speed to prevent vacuuming up something into the engine. Besides, blowing a tire by running over a sharp edge of old concrete would also be a disaster.

"Those A-10's are closed cockpits now. They're launching," said Kyle.
"How does he know that? Asked the copilot.
"He hacked their flight deck," said the pilot as he put his headset on and began surveying his own flight deck.
"Captain? If we take off and stay close to the mountains going North, we could make it to Palmdale and get lost in the commercial traffic."
"That's a good idea. We could stay on the deck over the Angeles National Forest right here, and then bank east along 14. It's possible."
Just then, Smith poked his head into the cockpit. "Here's the deal. Those A-10's have armed Hellfire missiles. Heat seekers. They also have 30 millimeter cannons which can rip this plane like paper Mache. The only thing they can't do is climb. They're slow and heavy, like a flying trash can. We have to make sure they can't get an angle on us."
"And how do we do that? We have mountains to the west, Lancaster to the north, and the only opening we have is here along 14 to 18. They have an angle, no matter how fast we fly. We can do about 375 at this altitude," said the pilot.
"If those A-10's get airborne now, there is no way we can make it," said the copilot.

"Okay. Okay. Okay." Stuttered Kyle as his brain came out of hacker mode. He twisted his reddish blond hair in his left hand while his right hand brushed across the pad on his laptop. "Here's your flight plan!" yelled Kyle from his swivel chair through the open cockpit door.

The pilot looked back at his flight deck. "What the hell? What is this?" he yelled over his shoulder. Smith winced at as the pilot yelled right in his face.

"Um. It's the flight plan. We can beat the A-10's and the Hellfire missiles if we follow this plan. I'm pretty sure," said Kyle sheepishly.

"This ain't no video game, kid. This jet cannot fly like this. This plan makes us fly straight up. We can't go vertical."

"It can now," said Dick. "Just do it."

"We will stall and fall back to the ground. I don't feel like dying today," said the pilot.

"I was looking over his shoulder, sir," said Jones. " He's way too fast for me, but I think it might work."

"Jesus Christ." The copilot directed the plane onto the end of the runway. 11 thousand 5 hundred feet of runway wide enough to launch a B-52 straight in front of them. He held the brakes so the plane stopped rolling.

"They're wheels up, sir," said the copilot.

"Okay. Here we go. Get in your seats you two." He picked up the mike. "We're firewalling it." He had not flown this way since flying cargo runs out of Riyadh in 1991. 6 thousand hours to end up like this.

Dick and Kyle looked at each other as the jet lurched forward like a sports car. It was off the ground in less than 3 thousand feet and wheels up. "200. 250. Pull back," said the pilot. Together, they worked the yoke of the plane. They had practiced 60 degree elevations coming off the runway lots of times. They had never done 90 degrees before.

"We're not fast enough, sir. Hold on. 300. 330. 350"

"That's good. We're at 6 thousand now. 400. Holy shit, what is that? That's not them. What is that?" spat the pilot over the DC's.

"That's a news helicopter. Evasive right. Hold on!" the pilot and copilot pulled back even more and guided the plane in a hard roll to the right. "Whoah! He went right, he went right. That guy has combat experience. Very quick. We're clear," said the pilot. The plane came back to the center and was now climbing at a 75 degree angle.

"Sir, two bogies at 320," said the copilot.

"I got 'em. They have an angle. They have an angle. They're going to fire."

"Go, go, go," wished the copilot.

"Now would be a good time, hacker boy," shouted the pilot.

"Pull up. Pull up. Three, two, one, go," shouted Kyle as he pressed F8 key.

At that moment the two jets released four Hellfire missiles. They dropped like bricks until the propellant ignited. They were AGM-114 heat seekers capable of reaching a speed of 950 miles an hour in level flight. The G-7 could fly at nearly the speed of sound in level flight, but they were climbing. They were practically vertical now, slowing down as time went on. The plane did not have enough thrust to go straight up and accelerate at the same time.

"Kyle?" asked Dick.

"Hold on."

"Kyle?"

"Hold on. I couldn't do anything until they dropped. Hold on."

"I'm going to have to dive to pick up airspeed. We're going to, holy mother of God," said the pilot as he gripped the yoke with all his might. The plane's GE engines were being doused with magnetized nitrous oxide. This mixed perfectly with the clean Jet-A kerosene fuel and produced a beautiful blue afterburning behind the jet. The passengers squeezed back in the seats while they gripped their armrests.

"400 sir. 500. 650. 750. Mach 1.1. Mach 1.2. Mach 1.5 Settling out. Sir, we just passed 50 thousand feet."

"Stay vertical. Follow the flight plan. We have about three more minutes of boost," said Kyle.

The oxygen masks dropped out of the ceiling. Nearly panicking, each person grabbed for a mask and put it on. The copilot was not so lucky. His mask fell behind him as they were pointed straight up. Within 15 seconds he was unconscious.

"We're at 75 thousand feet and still climbing. We're safe. I'm nosing over for level flight," said the pilot over the mike.

"No!" shouted Kyle. "If you do that we will explode. I cannot turn the nitrous off. It must run out."

"100 thousand feet. Hey hey, we're stalling. I need some help up here."

Dick released his belt as the plane began to feel very strange. He floated free of his seat and launched weightlessly toward the cockpit.

"He's out. He needs oxygen or he'll die," said the pilot.

Kyle popped his harness loose and grabbed his weightless body and threw it back toward Rhino. "Get a mask on him and belt him in."

"You da man," shouted Rhino through his oxygen mask. He grabbed the weightless copilot with one arm and slammed him onto the seat next to him. He attached the seat belt and put the dangling oxygen mask over his unconscious face.

"Oh my god," said Loretta. "Look!"

She hadn't made a sound during this entire flight, but now she was looking out the window of this jet from 100 thousand feet. She could see the curvature of the Earth. She could see the curvature of two Earths. One was holographic looking, but it was separating from the white and blue planet they called home. Her thesis was right, but witnessing it froze her heart in her chest. There were two Earths, one vibrating at a much higher frequency than the other, shining in various shades of blue outside the window.

They were in harmony, for the most part, for more than 5 thousand years. But now, just as her measurements and calculations had predicted, they were becoming dissident. The two worlds were going to come apart. It was like the planet was dying. Just like a human body dies. The physical part is temporal and slow and solid. The spiritual part was fast and as far as she could tell, eternal. The planet called Earth was a living thing.

Dick had the best view, for a moment. The enhanced optics out the cockpit windows made the picture absolutely stunning. He couldn't blink. It was beautiful. "Wow," was all that came out of his mouth.

"I know it's awesome and everything, but we have a serious problem," said the pilot. He had the yoke wrapped over the right as far as it would go, and he pushed it all the way forward. The plane, however, was beginning to fall backwards and spin to the left. Slowly, but the altimeter began spinning. "We've got almost no airspeed. We are going into a flat spin. These jets glide like a brick. I need some help with this elevator. Help me push this down."

Dick grabbed the yoke. Felt like a steering wheel. Two pedals. One goes right and one goes left. "What does this do?" he asked.

"That is the landing gear. Don't touch that."

"And this?"

"Reversers. Um. The engine cowl redirects the jet blast to slow the plane down once it touches down. Leave that alone or you'll kill us all."

"And these?"

"The engine throttles. Come on now, help with this, or we're going to spin out of control."

The plane was dropping fast at about 2 thousand feet a minute. 2 thousand five hundred. Once the stratospheric air began moving over the wings backwards, there would be no correcting it. They would spin so fast, they would pass out. The plane would soon shatter under the stress.

Dick grabbed the wheel hard and pushed in left into the spin. He reached forward and dropped the landing gear and then opened the reverse cowls on both engines. All that was remained was to, ah yes. The pedals. Push the right one all the way to the floor. The plane rolled upside down, the horizon came back into view and disappeared over the top of the cockpit window. Throttles. He reached for the throttles and shouted to the pilot, "Light it up. Light it up."

The pilot pushed the glow plug switches to light the engines. The compressors began turning. They could hear the ignition of the port engine, and the light went green on the flight deck.

"We have engine one," said the pilot.

Dick centered the yoke and pulled back slightly. He let up on the pedals and let them come to the center with the rudder. He closed the reversers and raised the landing gear.

"We have number two. Throttle up. 450. 550. 750. Okay, we have to level out and glide a little. These aren't made to fly too much past Mach 1."

They both sat there for a moment. They realized at the same time that they were going to live. The plane was saved. "Come around to 320. We're going to Camp David," said the pilot. "How did you know how to do that? I've never faced that before."

Dick turned his face to meet the pilot's and pointed to his patched eye. "Try crashing every night," he said flatly.

Chapter 14

The Gulf of Mexico is hot and humid most of the time, but once you get a few miles off shore, there aren't any bugs. Every once in a while, a breeze comes by that helps the sweat cool off the body. There are more than 25 thousand oil rigs in the Gulf. Most are rusty old wrecks, long since abandoned, but no one does anything about them. They get pounded by storms, and sea birds use them for respite, which makes most of them appear covered in bird crap.

But the Deepwater Horizon was one of the most modern rigs ever built. It had every safety device. It had excellent living quarters for the crew that operated it. It produced more oil than just about any rig ever built in the Gulf area. It was also the summer job for one Orphan Bayazed.

He was just 19 years old. That made everyone on the rig nervous. There wasn't any dead weight on an oil rig. Slackers were known to have accidents. It is a dangerous, slippery, stationary ship in one of the deepest and most temperamental seas on Earth. More than 700 Spanish barge chains loaded with gold have been sunk in storms on the Gulf. Thousands of roughnecks have been injured or killed on oil rigs all over that body of water.

But as dawn approached this Spring day, it was remarkably calm. The sea was as smooth as glass, and the sky was clear with the belt of Orion shimmering in the dark sky above. Orphan was on the first shift watch with his roommate, Judge. Some people called him 'the Judge,' but the name wasn't real. He was a Kelly technician, which was one of the most dangerous jobs on the rig. He also had been working rigs for more than 10 years. That was very rare for a roughneck. The work was filthy beyond compare, but the rig had to stay clean, especially the Deepwater. It meant lots of work and excellent pay. Two weeks on and two weeks off was a hard schedule for even young men, but it meant the company had to maintain two entire crews. They had to keep them safe on the rig, and they had to make sure they returned at the end of their two week shore time.

Orphan had a slight advantage that secured him a spot on the best paying rig in the British Petroleum fleet. His father grew up in the oil business, in Iraq and then came to the States when OPEC took control of the Middle East's oil producing capabilities and nationalized all the assets. He was able to move most of his assets as well, which enabled him to purchase the controlling interest in the Los Angeles Times. Ever since, the publication became an oil friendly organization. The relationship was good for both of them. And now, it would be good to Orphan.

The platform was 396 feet (121 m) long and 256 feet (78 m) wide and could operate in waters up to 8,000 feet (2,400 m) deep, to a maximum drill depth of 30,000 feet. Press releases from Transocean stated the platform had historically been used for deeper wells, including the deepest underwater gas and oil well in history at 35,055 feet. It was truly the finest rig on the sea.

The first shift starts at Midnight and goes until 8:00 AM. By then the sun is up and scorching, and it is a great time to hit morning mess and then go to sleep. So far, the Spring had been easy work. He was working in the monitor room that watched the blowout preventers and the stress on the rig anchors. It meant reports and rounds and clipboards and reading gages by hand. The Company had learned the hard way not to trust the remote monitor systems completely. They wanted human ears and eyes looking at things every hour. It meant walking each platform, from the sea all the way to the top towers. There were gages on top of the transducers that sent the pressures, temperatures, gas leak detectors, and strain values to a central computer screen. Operators would watch the screen to make sure the rig was operating within limits and making money. Patrols would validate the readings by filling out clipboards with the same readings from those local readouts. If they turned up different, the Bradley Bonner, a huge German master technician, sent maintenance to find out why the very next day.

Orphan and Judge had just finished walking more than one and half miles around the platforms and climbing more than 400 feet of stairs to reach the highest tower above the rig. The view was amazing on a clear night just before dawn. The sun would begin lighting the sky far from the horizon, making it turn a different shade of blue every single minute. Orphan would keep himself awake by forcing himself to try to see the horizon appear. One minute it would be washed in the blackness of the sea and the starlit sky. The next minute, there would be a slight edge of blackness next to a deep purple glow as the sun made its way around the planet. Sometimes the Geminids or the Leonids or the Perseids would splatter the dawn sky with meteors that could be easily seen without the light pollution of the city. It was magical. Even at the age of 19, he knew that life moves very quickly, and never let a night like this go unnoticed.

"It's kinda nice up here tonight," said Judge. He wasn't a man of many words. Orphan had tried many times to get him to talk about his experiences or give him advice on things. Most people considered themselves lucky if Judge said, "Eh," while passing him in a hallway or on a catwalk.

"Sometimes I think I'm like flying when I'm up here. I can hear birds or seals, or a boat blow its horn in the night. The stars are amazing," said Orphan. He was a football player in high school. He really didn't like working on the oil rigs in the Spring. It wasn't like he needed the money. But his dad wanted him to learn the value of a dollar. He wanted him to learn the business. Well, what he knew about it made him determined to have nothing to do with it as soon as he was able to make his own decisions in life.

He didn't wish this too loudly, though. His older brother had wished it one night when arguing with his dad about dating or street racing or something. He was sent to live with his uncle in Iraq when he graduated from school. They got mail from time to time. His brother regretted that argument. Orphan decided he was never making that wish aloud. He would work the rigs. This one was not too bad. It was new. It was state of the art. And it was very good money. He would be able to buy a new Harley Davidson after this summer.

There it was. There was the dark line between the sea and the deep purple sky. "Whoa. Look at that will you?" said Orphan.

"Another day another dollar," clichéd Judge.

"Yeah, you can say that again. How far do you think we can see from up here?"

"Oh, I guess about 20 miles or so," said Judge. "Sometimes you can see a supply ship an hour before it gets here."

"I am amazed how it will stay dark for so long, and then, like in 5 minutes the horizon starts getting light blue and then orange. And then it gets….hey…what is that?"

"What?"

"That. Those. Those two big humps."

"Um. Unless I'm hallucinating, that looks like a tidal wave."

"What? No way. We're in 5 thousand feet of water. Waves like those would be under the surface. Those are like, big," said Orphan with a squeak in his voice.

"Gimme that radio, kid."

Orphan handed him the walkie talkie clipped to his belt. They had never used it the whole time he had been on the rig, and he never really knew what to do with it.

"Control this is Judge," he said pressing the talk button. He waited about ten seconds, but Orphan could tell something was wrong. Judge had the most experience of anyone on that rig, and nothing rattled him.

They had a Hydrogen Sulfide alarm his first week there. It nearly made him piss, when it went off. Everyone was falling down and scrambling for the mask locker on the Kelly deck, which was the giant motor that turned the drill steel and supported more than two miles of drill pipe that stretched all the way to the bottom and then deep into a hole they had drilled to the oil and gas reserves trapped in volcanic formations. Hydrogen Sulfide is deadly poisonous. One breath will put you on your knees and make you see stars. The next breath, and you are unconscious. Within two minutes, you are dead. It normally comes up through the drilling mud that keeps the high pressure from blowing through while drilling, but this rig used blowout preventers, which captured the pressure deep under the sea where the water pressure could help contain the gasses. It made the rig very clean, and very dangerous to operate. Judge simply took a breath, walked over to the locker, and put his mask on like he was donning a ball cap. Then he helped others get their masks and put them on. Each mask is fitted to the roughneck's face when he first arrives, during orientation. The wrong mask could get you dead.

"Control. Come in" repeated Judge.
"Go ahead Judge," said the gravelly voice on the other end.
"Sound the alarm. We have a wave."
"A wave? There is no storm. Radar shows it's smooth as...oh hell...."
The alarm went off like a rock concert has just been plugged in with the volume on full blast. Orphan gripped the railing because he felt like the sound would knock him to the surface, 400 feet below.

"Follow me," said Judge. He put two hands on the hand rails of the metal stair in front of them, and swung his feet up in front of him onto the rails as well. Judge slid down 20 stairs in about three seconds. Orphan was too scared to try it, even though it looked easy enough. He wished he had time to practice something like that, when the alarm wasn't piercing his eardrums in the predawn darkness. He shuffled his new boots down the stairs, but Judge was already running along the catwalk for the next stairs. They had about 300 feet to go to reach the Kelly deck. "Come on. Move your ass rookie," shouted Judge.

The doors flung open from the dorm building and men began pouring out. Some had pants on only and were struggling to put their boots on. The deck was painted diamond plate steel, and it was no place for bare feet. The edges of the four by eight sheets were sharp and could easily lacerate bare skin. Bonner emerged like a Viking. His red helmet was strapped on and he was fully dressed. Orphan wondered for second if he slept that way, but then he realized that second shift was starting for maintenance at 7 AM, just two hours away. He came from breakfast, which he did not get to eat.

The rig began to move slightly at first. Orphan couldn't believe it. This rig weighed thousands of tons, and it was stabilized by eight sea anchors with automatic tethers. The first swell touched the bottom of the Kelly deck making the entire rig shudder like giant fingers strumming the pillars. The sound was deep and sickening like steel was no match for water. He could hear equipment slamming against the welded plates of the deck from underneath. Glass was breaking somewhere.

Orphan was far behind Judge now. Bonner was barking and pointing with one hand as he grabbed men like little kids and threw them with the other hand. "To the boats. Get to the boats. Don't worry about that. Abandon ship," he bellowed.

The rig was listing badly now, and he was thankful he wasn't up on that tower. It was whipping like a fishing rod up there near Orion's belt. He was nearly to the Kelly deck now. Just two more stair cases to go. There was an enormous rumble below as the second swell rocked the entire rig back the other way. It was the casing of the well. It was failing far below the surface. He knew in a few seconds the full force of thousands of pounds of gas pressure would burst to the surface. There would be oil. There would be methane. He worried that he could not hold his breath, because he was scared, and he was running. He threw his feet up on the rail and slid down the next set of stairs. This was the long run. He had to run all the along the west side of the rig, turn the corner and run another 50 yards to reach the next set of stairs that reached the Kelly deck.

He looked over the inside rail and could see Judge was running toward Bonner. Two old salts, he thought. They would get everyone off. Just then, the corner of the dorm building blew away in a giant fireball. It was silent for a second or two, and then the heat and sound reached him. He tried to shut his eyes and hold onto the rail, but he could not miss the prefabricated wall section strike Judge mid step and wipe him from existence. It smashed through the transfer pump cage and took the far corner of the rig out to sea about 200 feet.

He opened his eyes and could see Bonner struggling to his feet. His helmet was gone, and there was some blood on his face, but he was still shouting and still grabbing and still pointing. Like a captain going down with his ship, he ordered every man to safety. And then, as though he could read Orphan's mind, he looked up and saw him gripping the yellow steel hand rail like it had electricity coursing through it. "Get down from there. Come here, right now!" he shouted like a giant.

Orphan tossed himself toward the stair case and swung his feet over the rails and slid to the Kelly deck. He hit the deck running and reached Bonner in what seemed a few seconds. Bonner gripped him by the shoulders, and he felt like a little boy in his control. His hands were like iron, and he felt like nothing could move him from this spot, not even the fire.

"Let's go," said Bonner.

He probably knew his dad. Maybe. It seemed like he was under special care, as they ran toward the stairs that lead to the docks far below the Kelly deck by the edge of the rig. There were zodiacs in dry dock all the time. They were fueled, stocked with emergency supplies and first aid kits. They were lashed in place, but they could be untied and could be slid into the water and boarded in less than a minute. There was enough for both shifts, in case they had to abandon the rig during a shift change. That was a best practice shared with the Deepwater. There were thousands of ghost rigs out there in the Gulf. And there were ghosts on those rigs. Lessons learned. And the Company spared no expense to make sure the staff could get away safely.

They ran as fast as they could, which was like running in molasses. The smoke was getting thick now, as the oil from below mixed with the fire raging with natural gas. They could see the chaos below them. The zodiacs had mostly been strewn around by the two giant surges that came through at perhaps 100 miles an hour. It was like two semi trucks had slammed through the place. There were clouds of smoke and heat making everything slick and black.

Orphan coughed and tried to take a deep breath as Bonner grabbed another man who had fallen. "Get those boats in the water," he bellowed. It echoed off the floor above them and off the water 40 feet still below them. The men looked up and noticed Bonner. One man ran over and busted the glass on a case on one of the twisted support pillars. He retrieved an axe and ran to the boat, still lashed to its ramp, ten feet above the water. He chopped the ropes and the boat slid into the water. The motor and entire back of the zodiac submerged for a few seconds, and Orphan panicked thinking the boat would sink. But it bobbed back to the surface and started to drift away from the rig. Two more men jumped from ten feet above the surface and grabbed the edge of the Zodiac. They pulled themselves into the boat while a dozen more crew members jumped into the water for that boat.

He chopped another and another, each one filling with men and drifting away from the rig. "Stick together. The rescue boats will find us if we stick together," shouted Bonner. Orphan could hear the starters trying to start the big black Mercury motors on the back of each Zodiac. They were brand new, top of the line four stroke 200 horse motors. Always the best, Orphan thought.

There were still 200 men hanging off the rails below, waiting for boats to hit the water. "Get down there, son," said Bonner as he turned at looked at him with the same look his coach used to give before saying, "Get me that football, son." He hit the stairs and slid down to the boat deck below. Bonner stayed on top so that he could order the chaos from above. The men could hear him, and they felt like he was watching over them.

The next explosion took four pieces of diamond plate and ripped it from the deck. It twisted the stair off at the bolts like they were made of plastic, and slammed them into the sea below them. There was a boat, Someone pushed him, and he was in the water. He couldn't swim for some reason, and had a hard time making the surface after plunging from ten feet above the water. He was holding his breath, but then he realized he still had his boots on. He remembered snorkeling for fish off La Jolla one time and he kicked off his fins. He only had his rubber booties on so he could climb the rocks to get out of the water. A wave washed him back away from the rock, and the rubber booties just slipped through the water as he kicked, but didn't do any good for propulsion.

Same thing, he thought. He pulled hard with his arms and reached the surface to take a breath.

He stroked to the boat a few feet away. There was fire on the water not far away. The alarm had quit. It was probably blown away. The men in the boat already pulled him in. He was amazingly weak, he thought. He looked up on the twisted boat deck, and there was no one. His heart sunk, and then he heard that voice. It was lacking in its power, but it was there. "Stay together, and go west away from the rig. Stay away from the burning oil." It was Bonner. He was on another boat about 50 feet away. They were going to live. The Mercury rumbled to life and the boat surged out to follow the other boats already under way. The sun was cresting the horizon, and except for the dark billows of smoke pushing east, there was not a cloud in the sky.

Chapter 15

They were quiet as the company shuttle bus arrived at the tall, glass building just off highway 90. Gulfport, Mississippi was a small town, by national standards, but the oil industry ran an enormous operation from is sandy and wind-blown streets. Hurricane Katrina had devastated the oil industry just south of here in 2005. New Orleans had rebuilt much of the heavy infrastructure, but it became necessary to relocate the offices to Gulfport during that time. It was a major investment, and the company just felt like the cost of operating from here was better, so they stayed.

Orphan sat in the back in his yellow and green jump suit with the BP flower over the left breast. He was still sore and his throat was slightly burning from inhaling the oily smoke. He stood with the others and stepped onto the white sidewalk and up the marble steps of the BP office complex. The group walked quietly through the opulent lobby and divided up between three elevators to reach the 18th floor.

They walked down the carpeted hallway to the large, glass wall on the left and into the conference room. It was nice, Orphan thought. One table about 30 feet long with black leather chairs all the way around. Two men in suits were at the far end, and one man in what looked like a blue flight jacket. It was short at the waste and had a large round emblem on the right side. He wore sunglasses, even though they were inside. His arms were folded as they stood there waiting for the men to find a seat around the table.

Bonner took a seat next to him. He had a white cast on his left arm, and there were wires holding two of his purple fingers together. He winced as he placed it on the table in from of him. Orphan leaned back in his chair and noticed it reclined easily. He folded his hands across his stomach.

"Gentlemen, welcome to this meeting. My name is Brad Sorrensen. I am head of BP accident management. This is a debriefing of the events of two days ago on the Deepwater Horizon. You each have had the finest care available, and have been well attended to. Yes?" he asked holding his left hand out as though to urge a response.

"Yes." And "You bet," were some of the simultaneous replies. Orphan did not move. He was watching the three men. They had not let him speak to his father after they were rescued. He knew his father had seen the news. He had to. He owned one of the most powerful newspapers in the world. He knew his father was trying to find out if he was okay. They tried to take his cell phone, but he told them he didn't have one. He kept the battery out of the phone, because his dad said people might try to trace him someday. Because of him.

"BP is committed to cleaning up this spill as quickly as possible. I know the news makes it out to be an environmental disaster like the world is going to come to an end, but I assure you that within 60 days there will not be a trace of this spill anywhere to be found. After all, oil is natural too, and there are all kinds of critters that come out to break it down and live off it for a while." He paused and looked around at the table.

"This is Harold Hoffstetter. He is in charge of human resource development. He has a report and some forms you need to look over. Harry?"

"Believe me, gentlemen, nothing pleases me more than to see you here in good health," he began. "Let me read this, and then I will hand it around to you. At approximately five twenty on April 20th, 2010, the main blowout preventer on the Deepwater Horizon failed, causing a high pressure gas leak. This leak caught fire when it reached the surface and resulted in an explosion which destroyed the rig, killed 11 workers and injured 16 others. We, the crew of the Deepwater Horizon, add our testimonies that the blowout preventer was the root cause of the failure of the rig."

"While Harry is passing this around, I want to assure you that your positions are secure with the company. You all will be compensated for your hardship and experience and will be provided the first and best opportunities available to find work," said Brad.

"That's not what happened," the words escaped Orphan's mouth before he knew he had said them.

The two suited men looked at Orphan, and the third man unfolded his arms. It was the first move of any kind he had made. "Excuse me?" asked Brad.

"That is not what happened. There were these giant waves."

"Hold on, son," interrupted Bonner. "Guys, he's young and there was a lot going on that night," said Bonner in an uncharacteristically sweet voice. He held up his arm in the cast slightly and gestured. "Look, we have been through hell. There were waves everywhere. Don't pay any attention to my boy, here, He's cool." He gripped Orphan's shoulder with his right hand and looked into his eyes. Those cool, steel blue eyes were pleading with him to keep his mouth shut.

He had seen those eyes before in his mother's gaze as she begged him not to argue with his father. She had lost one son, and she did not want to lose him. It seems when an Iraqi marries an American woman, the sons are prone to strong tempers. His mother kept his in check. She was a blessing in his life, and right now he missed her more than anyone else.

"Yeah. It was a mess," said Orphan. He slowly picked up the pen without looking up at Brad or Harry and signed the paper that was placed in front of him.

"Gentlemen, thank you very much," said Brad. "Harry's got vouchers for you. These are good at the two casinos for dinner and $500 in chips. Relax. We'll be back in touch in a couple of days. Be safe out there," said Brad as he gathered the papers and handed them to the man with the sunglasses.

They each stood and walked single file out of the room. There were two vouchers left on the table.

Chapter 16

He couldn't sleep. The events of that afternoon were making him mad. The man walking up and down the hall had not shown up in a while. He felt he could go for a walk and feel better. Besides, he hadn't spoken to his father. His duffle bag had a pouch of quarters. He opened it, took out a handful, and stuffed them into his left jeans pocket. He didn't feel like wearing his BP jumpsuit. He grabbed his shoulder bag.

They were smart in putting them all on the 5th floor of the casino. There was only one way down, other than the stairs, but who wanted to walk 5 flights of stairs? "Me," he thought. He quietly closed the door and walked away from the elevators toward the snack room. He reached the access door to the stairs and gently opened it, slipped into the stairwell, and checked the door knob to make sure it would open to let him back onto the 5th floor. It worked. He closed the door behind him.

When he reached the ground floor, he cracked open the door and peeked. There was a BP jump suit standing by the front desk talking with the girl behind the counter. 'Slimeball,' he thought. He decided to walk down another floor to the parking deck below. He opened it and peeked. No one. He checked the door to makes sure he could get back in. No luck. It was blank. He looked around the stairwell and noticed a trash can. He took the swivel lid off the can and fished around a little, finding a card stock flier. He folded it down to a stiff little square and tore off the rest, discarding it.

He opened the door again and stuffed the little square into the latch hole. He closed the door, and pulled on it again. It opened without turning the handle. Perfect. He exited the stairwell and walked toward the street level ramp. There was no one in the booth. It was about midnight. 'Sleepy for a little town like Gulfport, wide awake for a casino,' he thought.

He reached the sidewalk and acted natural, like he was taking a stroll around the town. Within two blocks, he started breathing normal again. He turned right and saw a Circle K store a block away. 'Pay phone,' he thought. He reached the booth in about 5 minutes and reached in his pocket for the quarters. He knew the number. It was a special number they used in games. His father used to practice these games with them when they were little boys, and they both knew that dad wasn't always a good guy.

When the oil industry was captured during OPEC, the higher ups that worked with the American oil companies were taken out and shot. Billions in rigs, wells, and equipment was seized by Iran, Iraq, Libya, Saudi Arabia, and Kuwait. They colluded and fixed the prices as though all that oil equipment belonged to them. His father had escaped with millions. They had been looking for him ever since. And they had been looking for his boys.

"It's me," he said almost bursting into tears. He knew better. His dad knew the game.
"Are you alright?" asked his father in Farsi.
"I am unharmed, Father," he responded in kind.
"Do not tell me your location. Do you have your phone?"
"Yes."
"In one hour, put in the battery for 5 minutes. 5 minutes only. Then remove it and destroy it. Get rid of it. My man will come to get you."
"Dad?" but he had already hung up. The call lasted for only a minute. It was the game. He left the booth with a hole in his heart. He was trying to be strong, but he wanted to tell his dad what happened. He wanted to tell him that they were lying, that he had seen something that no one should have seen. No one could have seen that except him, he thought.

77

They were 48 miles from shore. There were only two men in the world that saw these waves, and one of them was dead. He wanted to tell him. He knew then, that he could not return to the hotel.

He started walking north away from the Circle K. He crossed the street and travelled perhaps 6 blocks. It was a cool, Mississippi night and the walking made him feel better. He saw a Motel 6 sign two blocks further up the road. No one would think a Bayazed would stay in a Motel 6, he thought.

He walked into the lobby and rang the bell. The old man was courteous, but he could tell that his middle eastern appearance was going to bring suspicion. It always did. "How are you doing," he said in his most California accent. "Can I get a room, please?"

"License and credit card," said the old man as he placed the clipboard on the counter for him to fill out. He opened his shoulder bag and got his wallet. He placed his California license and a credit card his father had given him for emergencies on the counter in front of the old man. The names matched, so there wasn't going to be a problem there.

"Hey, I don't have a car with me tonight. Is that okay?" he asked leaving the automobile information blank. "I am flying out tomorrow. Is there a shuttle?"

"No shuttle," the man said.

"Okay. That's cool."

"Room 205. Around the side here and up the stairs. Sign please."

"Thank you," said Orphan as he slid the license and card back in his wallet and zipped his shoulder bag closed. He knew that using this card would set many things in motion now. There would be movement. His father would know what to do.

He climbed the stairs, noticing that his left leg was sore from the ordeal on the rig. Maybe he had strained it. They would find his jumpsuit in his room tomorrow. He knew someone else would be searching for him as well. His card key opened the door, and he went inside. "Even this bed is going to feel good tonight," he thought. He sat down and remained still on the edge of the bed for a moment. His mind was racing. He was trying to think clearly now.

He unzipped the small pocket on his shoulder bag. He slipped his fingers behind the flap and felt the hidden slot. He peeled it open past the carefully sewn in Velcro and retrieved the thin cell phone and battery. Opening the back, he slipped the battery in place and noticed the time on the hotel clock. He did not turn the cell phone on. There was no need. In five minutes he would remove the battery and toss the phone in the trash in the back of the hotel. He would sleep lightly tonight.

Chapter 17

Abdulla Bayazed did not run the Los Angeles Times. He owned it. Still, the idea of compiling one of the largest newspapers in the world with everything from financial reports to the obituaries was fascinating. He was an insatiable reader and had devoured the ancient books as well as modern works on the origin and destiny of the Earth. He bought the controlling interest for one main reason; to stay in the light of the public eye. The people that were angry at him for escaping the sword of Islamic justice back in the early seventies were mostly dead now. Either old age or the other edge of that sword had caught up with them. They had sons, and their sons had sons, and the task of judging him had been passed down, along with the inheritance in a global power that was as old as the Earth itself.

In the ancient times, they were born with a mission. Some say they were the offspring of Eve, but not Adam. In the Garden, there was more than one suitor, say the ancient records. The first loved her more than air. The second lusted for her and beguiled her, and from that first union came the seed that gave roots to the evil that rose to power, and fell, and rose again, all by the power of the sword.

Adam fathered the higher man. To this seed was given the dominion over the Earth, by the Creator. As long as there was a father to tell a son about the eldest son's inheritance that was robbed from their forefathers, there would be soldiers willing to sacrifice everything to destroy that treasure for everyone.

Somewhere in the shadows, the dark prince that beguiled the virgin in the Garden spoke to his children. He gave them secrets. He told them about weapons and how to create currency and how to manipulate them to rule the world.

He gave them power in this earthly life beyond measure, and promised them limitless bounty if they could destroy Adam's children. He spent thousands of years tempting them, and betraying them, and luring them into his game of material wealth and slavery so that their souls would be lost to the Creator.

It was the true war of wars. It was fought on every world in every galaxy throughout the universe. And the dark prince was winning on every world, inasmuch as Abdulla could tell.

He read how worlds were put together capable of sustaining mortal life. They were formed of two parts; one spiritual and one temporal. And one day, it was prophesied, they would come apart and take their respective spirits with them. This grand separation would divide the children. So far, the more part of the people always remained with the temporal planets, doomed to starvation of the very spirit that gave them hope and joy. They would become hopeless and joyless, exactly like the children of the dark prince.

As he put down the phone that had never rung before this night, he felt the love for his son. He was afraid for him, but he knew that he had taught him well. His younger son was able to swallow his rage, unlike his brother. Orphan, he thought, was going to be a great man.

But first, he had to find out more about the Deepwater Horizon. Why had British Petroleum prevented him from calling home? Why had they sequestered the men from that rig? What happened was a tragedy. But, was it an accident? He had to find out, and he knew just where to start.

He sat down at his special terminal, tied into the firewalled resources of the planet's largest news organization. He started with the rig itself. Hmm, built in South Korea by Hyundai Heavy Industries in 2001, and owned by Transocean. It sank this morning in 5 thousand feet of water 48 miles off the Mississippi shore in the Gulf of Mexico. No evidence there.

Tony Hayward, the chief executive of BP, sold £1.4 million of his shares in the fuel giant weeks before the Gulf of Mexico oil spill caused its value to collapse. Goldman Sachs sold 4,680,822 shares of BP in the first quarter of 2010, less than 30 days before the explosion. Goldman's sales were the largest of any firm during that time. Goldman pocketed slightly more than $266 million if their holdings were sold at the average price of BP's stock during the quarter. It represented 44% of their total investment in British Petroleum, and more than 90% of its holdings in the Deepwater project.

"Hmm. That's very strange," he thought as the facts began loading. Halliburton bought an oil rig fire fighting company, Coots and Boots, just eight days before the Deepwater Horizon exploded. They paid $240 million for it. That's pretty high for a company that has not really made money in several years.

The more he researched, the more plain the story appeared. These people knew this was going to occur. There was more to it than the coincidence of just completing routine casing cement work by Halliburton on the well beneath the rig. The casing is temporarily cemented shut, or plugged, during this process to make sure the casing is secure through dozens of strata from the surface of the ground, all the way to the geological formation bearing the oil. Then, they just redrill through the concrete to open the well back up. This prevents contaminants from getting into the stream of oil making its way up to the pump, but it also prevents the oil from below from pushing into aquifers, where drinking water might be flowing.

The chances of this being the cause of the blowout were slim to none. He had drilled dozens of wells in Iraq, and knew the procedures very well. This service company had put out many well fires in Iraq during the 1990 Kuwait invasion when Saddam Hussein's Republican Guard torched the wells as they retreated. It made it even more bazaar that Halliburton would spend nearly a quarter of a billion dollars to buy a company that is only needed when there is a fire barely a week before they are needed on a rig that they had just finished casing.

Hmm. Says here that experts decided the sinking of the rig was caused by the firefighting team. Instead of using foam to extinguish the fire, they used seawater, overwhelming the ballasts, which flipped the rig and caused it to sink in more than a mile of water. 'Wow. That was clever,' he thought. Sinking the evidence in a mile of ocean was brilliant.

Still, it was the well casing failure that caused the rig to catch fire and explode. So, what made the well casing fail on such a calm, Spring morning in the Gulf of Mexico? It became clear to Abdulla Bayazed that the richest companies on Earth knew when it would happen. They used this knowledge to make themselves individually very rich. He also knew there was only one person who could tell the truth, and that person was his younger son.

It was then that he noticed the small icon appear in the lower left of his screen. The cell phone location information arrived. He had to act fast now. He picked up the phone that rarely rang. He dialed the number he rarely dialed. "Bayazed. I'm sending the location data now. Five hours? You have four. Go get him now. Thanks," he said curtly over the phone.

He wondered for a moment if he had done the right thing. He could have sent one of his bodyguards, but there was something wrong here on a much larger scale. Everything he could find indicated that the Deepwater was the finest rig of its kind in the world. The movement of so much money, the expensive insurance policies, and what seemed like the deliberate sinking of this billion dollar cash cow told him this, somehow, was being run from much higher up. Such planning to compensate for cosmic events that had not happened yet required a perspective that was older than humanity itself. That is why he called Hadid.

The Iron bar. He was unbreakable. Hadid's father had saved his life in Iraq, twice, and helped him make it to America at the cost of his own. Hadid was born in Charlotte, North Carolina and studied history at Chapel Hill. He entered the Secret Service at age 22 and has been assigned to nothing but presidents ever since. He had been taught what to look for from a very young age, which was very rare for a boy in modern times. Certain events were prophesied, and until they happened, the ancient order, to which Hadid belonged by birth, would lie in wait. He would know what to do. He knew his son would be safe now.

Chapter 18

"Are we there yet?" asked Shelly.

"We're going to fly down this ridge, and then we should have a view of the plateau," said Elvis. "If it's the old flight line I remember, we should be able to see it from there."

"Nose camera is recording. We're not live, guys. So far, no word from central," said Jimmy.

"This is Shelly Lasalle, coming to you live from where, I have no idea," Shelly said softly over the intercom headset. "My ass is killing me."

"We're turning to one eight zero."

"Hey, correct me if I am wrong, but are those Warthogs?" asked Jimmy.

"You are correct, reverend," said Elvis. "Those two are flying in combat formation, tight and low."

"Yeah, but they're not coming towards us, are they?" asked Shelly.

"Not exactly. I'm picking up targeting signals on my storm scope, though. They are targeting something south of here," said Elvis. "There it is. Looks like a drone. No, wait a minute, that is not a drone. That is a G-7."

"They're not going to shoot a G-7 in the California desert," said Jimmy flatly.

"Hang on, I'll turn toward it, so you can get it on camera. This might be interesting."

"Interesting? There might be people on that plane," said Shelly.

"Oh crap! They just dropped ordinance! Hellfires. Hang on," yelled Elvis. The G-7 was travelling at more than 375 knots. The Jet Ranger was now on a collision course with it at 140 knots, making the collision approach extremely fast. The CAS made an electronic siren noise that caused an instant reaction in Elvis. He had practiced this maneuver thousands of times in the simulator and twice in combat. He pulled back and to the right, sending Jimmy to the floor near the nose trim wheel in the center console and tossed Shelly's hair over her face. Shelly shrieked for a second and then choked it off as her head snapped forward.

"What the hell are you doing?" yelled Jimmy as he pushed himself back upright to sit in his jumpseat.

"Evasive action. We were going to collide with the G-7.

"Geeze, where is it?" said Shelly

"Turning to three two zero. There it is. The Hellfires are closing on it." Said Elvis.

"Can you get this on camera?" asked Shelly.

"I'm all over it." Jimmy said as he swung the nose camera joystick all the way to the left and up.

In a few seconds the G-7 pointed upward while the Hellfires corrected their courses to intercept. A pair of long blue, pointed flames poured out the rear of the white jet as it reached vertical.

"Sports fans? I believe those are," he paused for a second," "afterburners?" said Elvis pointing to the G-7 turning straight up vertical in flight.

"Isn't a G-7, like fancy, like a corporate jet?" asked Shelly.

"Correctomundo," said Elvis. "Hellfires are falling behind. That baby is gone."

The Hellfire missiles followed for a few seconds longer, until the white smoke sputtered and quit. They wobbled and went four different directions, and then began tumbling to the ground. Within a few hundred feet of the ground, they exploded in four balls of flame without making a sound.

"Did you get that?" asked Shelly like she was coming out of a trance.

"Oh yeah," said Jimmy with the same spacey tone.

"Let's go home before those A-10's decide we are lunch," said Elvis. He stepped on the left pedal and headed back for Pasadena over the San Bernardino Mountains. "I've been to a two-pie supper and a service station opening, and I have never seen anything like that before," said Elvis over the intercom. No one said another word, as they climbed out over Big Bear Lake, heading home.

Chapter 19

Dick had dozed off in the co-pilot's seat of the G-7, when he felt a hand on his shoulder. "Huh?" he said with a slight jerk.

"I got it from here, sir. Thank you for your help back there," said the co-pilot.

"Oh, that's okay. That was a wild ride," said Dick as he took the green DC headset off and handed it to the co-pilot and unfastened his harness.

"No kidding, son. That was amazing. I'm going to have to take up gocart racing now," said the pilot.

"No worries, cap," quipped Dick as he walked through the cockpit door and back to the cabin. Only Kyle and Loretta were awake. Rhino and Bett were asleep still with their oxygen masks on. He took a seat next to Kyle, and they smiled at one another. "We made it," said Dick.

"No thanks to number forty two," said Kyle. They fist bumped. That was Dick's number when his cart slammed into the wall that claimed his racing career.

"We were at the edge of space," said Loretta, catching both their attentions. She slipped her mask off, noting that Dick was no longer wearing his.

"Yeah, well I can dig being weightless, but we're cruising at 50 thousand feet now. Last time I looked, we had a hell of a tailwind up here. It won't be long now."

The cockpit was quiet at this altitude. Not much air was passing over the fuselage, and there was a slight, green haze to the front of the cockpit glass. "St. Elmo's fire," said the pilot pointing forward. It was an electrostatic effect of the stratospheric air passing over the glass that rarely made an appearance. The conditions had to be just right.

"How long has this been blinking?" said the co-pilot as he settled into his seat and put his harness on.

"Oh. I don't know. I didn't notice it a minute ago," said the pilot.

The copilot reached forward and turned the rotary switch on the radio to the blinking light. "Two six, four Quebec Romeo," said the copilot into the mike on his headset. They never said the "N" at the front of the serial number. Every plane in America had the letter "N" in front of the serial number. "Roger, stand by," he said. He flipped back to the internal intercom. "Smith? You have a comm. In the cockpit."

Agent Smith popped awake and removed his oxygen mask. He had a red mark around his square jaw where the elastic band had held the plastic bag against his face, saving his life. He unbuckled his belt and made his way holding onto the backs of the chairs in the short row of seats in the cabin. The copilot handed him the engineer's headset, and Smith slipped it over his ears. "Hello? Smith here."

"Hold on," said the copilot. He rotated the switch back to the blinking light.

"Hello? Smith here," he repeated. The sleepy look on his face turned to alert attention. "Yes sir. I will inform them. Do you need me to call you when we arrive? Got it. Yes sir." The blinking light went out. The copilot turned the rotary switch to the cockpit only circuit. "That was Hadid. Set a course for Gulfport, Mississippi. We have a guest to pick up."

"Yes sir," said the pilot. "Run the plan, but don't upload it. We're going in dark, 5777 transponder."

"Yes sir," said the copilot.

Smith returned to the cabin, where everyone was awake now.

"What's up?" said Jones like he had been asleep for two days.

"Slight detour," said Smith. "We have one more joining us."

"Where are we going?" said Loretta, concerned for the safety of her grad students.

"Gulfport, Mississippi. There was a witness to the event. The president wants him safe."

"There won't be any place that is safe, if my calculations are correct," said Loretta.

"There's room for error," chimed in Bett eager to protect her from Smith.

"That's not what I mean," said Smith. "There are others who know about this. They don't intend on your information reaching the president."

"Smith!" cautioned Jones.

"Hey. After what we just encountered, they deserve to know a little about what we're up against," retorted Smith.

"Yeah. We almost got wasted twice back there. Somebody wants us not to make it, don't you think?" said Rhino finally joining the conversation.

"Nice view, though. Wouldn't you say?" said Dick.

"I'll say. What was all that about," said Kyle. "I was kinda busy."

"It was the union of the polarity," said Loretta.

"There are two planet Earths," said Rhino. "One is vibrating very fast, kind of like a holographic version of the planet." And the other one,"

"The other one," interrupted Bett, "is just plain old rock and metal."

"They have been in harmony for thousands of years, and now, at the end times, they are coming back apart," explained Loretta.

"That's what that was?" asked Dick. "The two planets are coming apart?"

"Yes," said Loretta.

"So, why are we going to DC to see the president?" asked Kyle.

"There is much more to the story," said Smith. "That is why we are here. That is why we need to see Dr. Wesson's data that she left out of her thesis," Smith said stressing the last few words.

"So, I don't get it. If these two bodies were in harmony for so long, like music, you know. I love music and Cymatics theory. Way cool. What changed?" asked Kyle racing ahead of everyone else in the room. He noticed he had forgotten to say something. Like he had finished the thought, but forgot to tell everyone else. "I mean what changed? You know? For thousands of years, the music is cool, and then the notes go sour. What Changed?"

"Consciousness," said Loretta.

"Whose?" asked Kyle.

"Everyone's. There are 7 billion people on the Earth right now. They form an average state of energy."

"Oh yeah. Like a very large population of numbers, the statistics are very stable. I mean the average is stable. Hard to shift, though," Kyle said doing the calculations in his mind.

"Unless there is an outside force trying to shift it," said Smith.

With that, there was a pause in the room. Each person stared from person to person and back again until everyone had seen everyone.

"What does that even mean, Smith?" asked Bett, slapping her thighs with her hands. "You know, you have been nothing but a total pain in the ass since we met you."

"Bett!" shot Loretta.

"No, I'm sorry, boss. I am this close to finishing my doctorate," she said raising her voice and holding her finger and thumb close together, "and this has been a shit show from the get go. We have been chased, shot at, and nearly launched into space, thanks to Jimmy Jet over here. How can I get off this ride?"

"Yeah. When do we stop and get something to eat?" said Rhino. At that, everyone busted out laughing.

"Oh, man," said Dick.

"Nice one," said Kyle.

"Always thinking with your stomach," said Bett, much more relaxed now and trying to back her way out of bringing the entire cabin to a fever pitch.

"You da man," said Rhino.

"That reminds me. Got an ETA, Smith?" asked Jones.

Smith stood and walked to the cockpit. In a few seconds he returned. "Flight plan is done. We'll be descending in 2 hours. Better get some sleep. We have some more to go."

Chapter 20

Dick opened his eye with the soft jolt of the G-7 touching down at Gulfport International Airport. For the first time since the crash he slept without breaking into a cold sweat and hitting the wall. Perhaps he had finally resolved that challenge in his mind. He was calm inside, like he had the found the final piece to a puzzle he was working on the kitchen table.

The rest of the passengers woke up as the pilot tapped the brakes and taxied to the general aviation section of the airport. He pulled up to the hangar and shut down the engines. "We're going to need a few pounds of fuel," said the copilot.

"Smith?" queried the pilot as he took off his light green DC headset.

"Yes."

"We're going to need fuel. How long are you going to be?"

"Our coordinates are across the street. It is 4:21 AM now. We should be no more than 30 minutes if we have no troubles," said Smith. He motioned to Jones, who jerked the bottom of his suit jacket as though shaking out any wrinkles he might have gotten during the flight from Victorville. "We'll be back with our guest," said Smith. He rotated the handle on the door lock and pushed the air stairs down into the cool Gulfport humidity. He stepped out onto the top step and took a deep breath. It was quite a change from the arid high desert in Southern California. He shuffled down the steps and onto the tarmac. He needed a car.

Smith and Jones walked to the pilot's prep office. It was always open at General Aviation. Jets left and arrived at all hours from all over the world, especially since BP's Mississippi headquarters had moved here in 2005. A young man approached the counter as they walked into the lobby. "Good morning gentlemen. How can I help you?"

"We are just here to pick up an associate staying nearby. Would it be possible to rent or borrow a car?" asked Smith. The man looked at the two of them. Jones smiled calmly and tried not to look like he was assessing a threat or standing at attention.

"Well, the rental counter doesn't open for another two hours. Um. We have a station wagon. I can let you borrow that, it it's not going to be too long," said the man with a trusting voice.

That was southern hospitality, thought Smith. Two well dressed strangers walk in, and you just loan them your car. That would never happen in DC. "Thanks so much. We should be no more than 30 minutes. We're only going a couple of blocks. Can we bring you back anything? A coffee?" asked Smith as he reached for the keys being handed to him.

"No. That's okay. You need any fuel?" asked the man.

"Yes. As a matter of fact, our pilot is coming in now to make those arrangements. Thanks again. We'll be back soon," said Smith. He turned with Jones and headed for the station wagon parked outside the front door of the General Aviation office that faced the parking lot outside the secure airport perimeter fence. They would be scanned coming back in. That could be a problem, he thought.

"Let's go get our boy," said Jones.

The station wagon was old and ran like a top. It was discreet, he thought. No blinking blue lights or massive, bullet proof Escalade with a police escort. Nice and quiet and plain looking was the way to go this morning. "How are we doing?" asked Smith who was driving.

"Make a left at the light. We're close," said Jones looking at his smart phone with the tracking app running. He had the exact coordinates from the satellite, and a charge card record from Motel 6, so he knew what he was looking for. "There's the sign. Turn right up there and go down the back side." Smith killed the lights as he bounced into the Motel 6 parking lot. He went around to the front lobby and Jones got out. Smith stayed in the car. "I'll find his room."

He swung open the lobby door and noticed the clock on the wall. 4:30 AM. He rang the bell on the counter, and a young girl came around the wall dividing the back office from the counter. She smiled and said in a Mississippi drawl, "Good morning. Welcome to Motel 6. What can I do for you?"

"I am here to pick up a friend. His name is Orphan Bayazed," said Jones.

"Well, I will call his room and let him know," she said.

"Which room is it please, so I can help him with his bags?" asked Jones.

"Well, I am not supposed to give out that information," she paused with the receiver in her hand.

"It's quite alright, miss," he said with his hands softly on the counter in plain sight. "You can go with me and show me the door. You don't have to tell me anything. Okay?" giving the girl a choice that she tried to translate into action.

She could make sure her guest was alright. If there was trouble, she could call 911. She had never escorted someone to a room before, but he was so handsome and the suit was expensive, and he was young and sounded so educated. It would be fine. "Okay. It's just around the corner here. Come on," she said walking around the counter and leading him to the front door. They walked around the corner and up the metal stairs to the second floor walkway. They walked down to room 205, and she held out her hand. "Room 205. Here we are," she said in a soft southern voice as though not to wake anyone else who might be sleeping.

Jones knocked gently on the door. There was no light on. A few seconds later, the door rattled as the safety latch moved against the door opening slightly. "Mr. Bayazed? Your father sent me," said Jones.

"Okay," said Orphan. "Gimme a second." He was still tired. Only 3 hours sleep after all that had happened in the

95

last two days. He was groggy. He didn't know this man in the suit, but who else on the planet would know that his father was sending someone for him? He didn't look like a BP puke. They all smelled of oil anyway. Dad used to say that pungent, sulfur smell was the smell of money. But it was impossible to wash out of your clothes. They all smelled the same.

The door closed again, and the safety latch was moved away. "Well, I guess you'll be okay now?" asked the girl.

"Yes. You have been perfect. Thanks so much," said Jones extending his hand to shake hers.

His had was so warm, she thought. She smiled, and he could not see her blush in the darkness. "Ya'll come back," she said sliding her hand out of his.

That was the way to say good bye in the South, Jones thought. Spanish people wave backwards, which Americans think means *come here,* when they are actually saying the same thing with their hands. 'Ya'll come back.' "Made so much sense," reasoned Jones as he watched the girl's head disappear down the steps.

The door opened again, and Orphan had nothing but his shoulder bag. "That's it?" asked Jones.

"Let's go," said Orphan, resolving to be a man of few words this morning. "Silence is strength," his father used to tell him. "Say nothing, and be firm about it," he would say. He never understood that until this very minute.

Jones turned and walked swiftly toward the old station wagon. "What's this?" asked Orphan.

"Airport car," said Jones. "Get in."

"Whatever," said Orphan. He was feeling aggravated for some reason. Probably from no sleep. He sat in the back and closed the door as he sat behind Jones on the passenger side.

"I am Secret Service Agent Smith," said Smith as he turned around from the driver's seat. Your father asked us to pick you up. Are you alright?"

"Yeah. I'm okay. I just wanted to make sure, you know?"

"You're in good hands, Orphan," said Smith. "We better stop here and fill this car up and get something to eat."

"There's a Circle K right on the corner up there," said Orphan.

They pulled up to the outside pump and Jones got out to pump. "Stay in the car. Don't look toward those cameras. I'll be right back," said Smith. After a few minutes, the handle clicked off just as Smith was emerging from the store with two sacks of supplies. Jones put the handle back on the pump and opened the passenger door behind the driver's seat. Smith tossed the supplies on the seat, and Jones shut the door and moved quickly around to the passenger side while Smith got in. They had no time to waste. It would be light soon.

Smith tossed the keys to the General Aviation station manager behind the counter. "I filled it up for you," he said.

"Wow. Hey, you didn't have to do that," said the man.

"No. Think nothing of it. We're just returning the favor. Thanks for letting us use it," said Smith.

"No problem. Hey, safe flying. Ya'll come back."

That southern charm. 'One day he would retire,' he thought. Maybe the South was the place to be.

"Let's go. Wheels up. Let's go," said Smith as he, Orhpan, and Jones bounded up the air stairs with the supplies. Smith pulled the air stairs in and latched the door. He turned toward the cabin. "Everybody use the facilities? We're good to go?" asked Smith.

"Is that food?" asked Rhino.

"Animal," said Bett.

"Yes," said Jones handing the sacks to Kyle and Dick who were seated in the front two seats.

"Ah yes. Slim Jims," said Dick. He took two sticks and a Pepsi and handed the bag over his shoulder to Rhino.

"There's more in there," said Smith.

They each took something to stave off the hunger from the long night. The pilot could be heard negotiating with the tower for clearance to take off. There was no fog on the runway this morning, so they could leave right away. Smith felt safe for once. There was no chase. There were no missiles. No one was shooting at them. He relaxed for a moment and reflected on this strange mission and the wonderful people that occupied this cabin at this time. Sure beats a plane load of drunken politicians making deals with other people's lives.

He took a seat next to Jones and extended his hand. "So far, so good," he said returning Jones' strong grip. "Next stop, Camp David," he said as he leaned his head back and closed his eyes for what seemed like the first time in days.

Chapter 21

Six a.m. came earlier than usual for the new president. Riker had barely closed his eyes after the meeting deep below the White House with Hadid, John, and Enoch. Just when he was coming to terms with the reality that he had won the most improbable election in history, the weight of what they had told him changed everything. This was perhaps the final generation of people on the Earth. He actually enjoyed the challenge of politics and the campaign solutions he had recorded on YouTube and used to fill in the content gap that formed in the wasteland between the two parties.

It had only been a couple of months, but he was already beginning to like this job. He was able to help people and prevent calamity between nations. He had already spoken to the leaders of Russia, China, Germany, and various special interest groups in the US. His ideas for making the world a better place had little to do with feeding the needs of these people. It had much more to do with actually dismantling the power the agencies had over the world. After all, the secretaries worked for him, and they ran each of the agencies, departments, bureaus, and administrations. If he told them to stop enforcing certain aspects of their regulations, they had to do it. It was a good place to start, he thought.

His first meeting this morning was with the Joint Chiefs. Seasoned military guys from each branch of the national defense. There was enough power in that room to destroy the whole world a few times over.

"Mr. President," they all said in some sort of unison as he entered the room. It was a sign of respect, but he came to terms with the fact that they did not really respect him. Well, maybe the Admiral did. When he shook his hand, he seemed to mean it. Admiral Samuel Denetti expressed his concern over coffee once about his whole force being exposed at sea in international or even hostile waters.

Sam and Robert looked at one another when the intelligence briefing they attended revealed that the Chinese had a surface to surface missile type drone that could cruise at 600 miles an hour and then, suddenly accelerate to 4 thousand miles an hour just yards off the surface of the water. At that speed, ship radar would only have about 20 seconds to lock on and fire countermeasures. If this modern-day Kamikaze drone was in the process of accelerating, it was nearly impossible to intercept. They were capable of carrying nuclear warheads as well. That meant that if the warhead detonated within a mile of the ship, they were all dead. If it hit the ship, it would take 45 minutes for the sea water to fill in the hole left behind. There was a mutual bond after that coffee.

"The world is a dangerous neighborhood," said the four star general Daniel D. Cabarrus. The US Army seemed to be transforming itself again. They had Rangers and Special Forces and something the CIA called Special Action Agents that made them operate more like assassins than soldiers. Presidents had been asking for a killing machine with no fingerprints for a long time.

Riker's father had told him when he was young to never trust someone who would steal for you. His gut told him to never trust someone who would assassinate for you. He guessed there was a reason why historical armies lined up and shot at one another or charged at one another across the frozen tundra with battle axes. There was honor in that style of fighting. Still, he shuddered at the thought of being immersed in that much fear and that much anger and blood all day, every day, until the leader of the other side turned his horse around and went home. The records were full of wars like this lasting for years or even decades.

Something, or someone kept them breeding and training more soldiers. Each era, the weapons on one side would match the weapons on the other side, and they would fight until the mothers of lost sons would pressure their leaders that they could bear no more. The dark prince's progeny mastered the art of complete female suppression. The Seed of Lucifer would capture and mutilate children and then deny any access to education. They would beat anyone who spoke out against them or complained and then celebrate public executions for girls or women who opened their mouths against their husbands.

They were taught the value of oil and the skill of bribery and deception. Within a few generations, men and women learned to make themselves exceedingly wealthy from these dark lords and their blood stained gold and diamonds. They sold their districts, and their cities, and their States, and finally their countries for a short lifetime of wealth and power.

For a while, it seemed, there were men of honor who would discover these syndicates and put them in jail or execute them for treason. But those men grew old and tired. Within a few decades, the reign of the judges was secured behind a system of bribery and compromise. They would issue their rulings as instructed by the agents of the dark prince. Faithful people were executed or targeted by various government agencies for malicious litigation or acts of terrorism perpetrated by their own government. It became apparent that nothing could be done to stop them.

So these briefings with the Joint Chiefs were formal and scheduled and completely ineffectual. At times, he felt like he was being sold the next regime change or the next trillion-dollar weapons system that would give them an advantage in the neighborhood. "What is your biggest fear?" he had asked them once.

"You mean who do we fear the most?" they responded.

"Yes. I mean we have been fighting a bunch of mountain men on old Honda 125 motorcycles and with used, unarmored pickup trucks with untrained gunners standing in the back. They have no tanks. They have no airplanes. They have no ships. They barely use radios. They have no satellite intelligence or Joint Chiefs. And yet they have been kicking your asses for 30 years. You seem to like it, because the checks are still cashing. Who do you really fear? The Russians? The Chinese? The Indians?" He was emotional and realized that they had been yelled at before by presidents. They would lock shields, it seemed, to protect one another and not let any one person be singled out for that ass chewing.

"Well. No, Mr. President. What we have, they have. What they have, we will have soon. The biggest fear is the American people."

He was shocked to hear this from Cabarrus. Admiral Denetti looked at him. Riker looked at him. "I'm not sure I understand."

"No, you wouldn't, sir," he said leaning forward now. "Leadership is about control. All those battlefields you mentioned are in control," he argued.

"In control? You come in here on a weekly basis and tell me of casualties and budget items, and skirmishes and sorties, and you say this is all in control? When did it become alright to maintain an endless battle, and never have a war? When did it become the goal to continuously fight and never seek surrender? Peace is supposed to come after victory, gentleman. When are we going to have victory?"

"It never has worked like that, sir," spat Cabarrus. "The great war didn't end all wars. It just ended wars like those. We don't fight uniforms anymore. We fight ghosts. We fight preachers and zealots. Our steel and titanium is useless against them. Sometimes I feel like the British felt when this nation was formed."

"What is that supposed to mean?" asked Riker, leading him into his own resignation.

"The British commanded the finest, richest, and most well-armed fighting force on Earth at the time. The colonies mustered an army of farmers and lumberjacks. They changed the way war was fought for thousands of years. They hid behind trees and hid behind children and women in plain sight. They shot soldiers in the back, poisoned their water, and wore them down over a period of years by leading them into the wilderness and slaughtering them. Does that sound familiar?" retorted Cabarrus.

"I see what you're saying," capitulated Riker. Cabarrus was not as dumb as he looked. He was battle hardened and had more medals on his chest than he could fathom, but it appeared he was a historian as well. Patton, he thought. Great movie. Sad end to a brilliant warrior. He could hear the frustration in the general's voice. He was at a loss what to say. "You said you feared the American people, a minute ago. Why?" asked Riker.

"I'm not afraid of them for me, Mr. President. I am afraid of them for you. We will just be called to fight the war," he said.

"Me?"

"Not you, per se'," entered Denetti. "There are really two governments in our country. One is elected. They get the blame when things go badly. And you, Mr. President. You get the blame, too," he began. "Then there is the other government that really took form in 1933 with Roosevelt. You remember the Crash." Denetti was going to tell a story, so Riker slumped slightly in his chair. He realized he had been stiff and tense the entire time Cabarrus was talking.

"Today, there are more than 655 agencies, all of which write regulations that have the force of law. They tax and fine, confiscate property, and rule over the people and consume 90% of the national budget. And none of them are elected. That, Mr. President, is taxation without representation. Tyranny. And the American people still will not tolerate tyranny."

"And there are 150 million of them, all armed, many hundreds of thousands of them trained by us," said Cabarrus. "You think we have problems with a few thousand insurgents on mopeds with an AK-47? Wait until the citizens begin marching on the capitol," said Cabarrus coldly.

"That's never going to happen," said Denetti.

"My sources tell me otherwise, and we need to be prepared."

"Prepared to do what?" asked Riker.

"Just prepared, Mr. President," said Cabarrus stiffly.

"If you're saying that federal troops would ever be used against the American people on American soil, I believe that is not constitutional," said Riker.

"Yeah? Well, insurrection is also mentioned in that document. When a governor asks for help from the president to put down an insurrection, you have to send in federal troops to put it down," said Cabarrus.

"Oh, like Lincoln? That was called an insurrection too, you know," responded Riker.

"Well, now at least you're getting the picture, Mr. President," said Cabarrus with an edge to his voice.

"Okay. Listen up," said Riker. "I believe I was elected because the people were tired of the old one party system. They were tired of the wholesale invasion of this country for the last 30 years by people who just strolled across our borders. They are tired of the spending, and the perception that Washington was taking away their liberty and offering an IOU on security. Now, you're trying to tell me that the real threat to America is the American people? Well, I'm not buying it. I can tell you it is hard to get the American people to get together on anything or come out for anything, let alone vote. But when they do come out in masses, we are not going to fight them. We are going to listen to them, because they probably have a legitimate grievance. The fact that they are armed is supposed to remind us that it is our job to listen to them. We are serving at their pleasure." Riker knew he was right, but he wasn't changing the minds at this table.

These men were stalwarts in their religions of war and using force or the threat of force to achieve their goals. He feared the only thing he had accomplished was establishing himself as their enemy as well. Especially general Cabarrus. He glanced up at Hadid, scanning the room from the edge of the wallpaper in the room. He had perhaps heard these words before with other presidents. Maybe not. Maybe he had heard worse. He wondered if there would be another predawn coaching session in the bowels of the White House. "Thank you all for coming," said the president.

No one said another word as they stood and left the room. He was at least secure in the thought that the codes to launch any kind of weapon rested with him. The thought made him cold inside, but he was convinced now more than ever that there was great wisdom to be revered. "That kind of wisdom does not come from men," he thought. Now, the only thing he had to do was not be tricked into betraying that wisdom.

Chapter 22

"What's on the agenda?" Riker asked his chief of staff. Actually, she was the previous president's chief of staff, but she knew the system better than anyone. In a way she was a lifesaver, because she kept all the time wasters away and let him know who was supposed to have access to him and who wasn't. Access, in the presidential world as it turned out, was bought and sold. It was sold by the chief of staff, and it was bought by donors.

So, over the centuries, both of them, the precious seconds of the president's time allowed him to see and hear only that which the chief of staff allowed him to hear. The only time he had to himself, it would seem, was when he was in the shower and when he was asleep. Or when, he was supposed to be asleep.

"You have some legislation to sign, two to veto, and then you have to fly to Florida to help the governor there keep his position. I have your speech right here for you to read, and it will be uploaded to the teleprompters in Orlando," she said like she had the whole next month planned out.

"Legislation? Shouldn't I read it first? I mean what is it about?" he asked.

"These were passed before you were elected. They take a little while to make it to me, and they are now ready for your signature. I just assumed.." she began.

"Margery," he interrupted. He wanted to call her Madge because she looked like an old TV commercial about dishwashing liquid or something, "if you don't mind, I will read these tonight and make a decision in the morning," he said. "What's this one?" he asked holding up the top printed and bound document.

"Mr. President, if you take the time to read these, we will never get anything done. These were written by experts and processed through Congress and the Senate," she explained.

"I'm pretty sure that is backwards," he said. "Bills are written by Congress and passed, then sent to the Senate and passed, and then to the president for approval. They are not crafted by corporations, printed and bound and then sent to Congress for their thumbs up. No wonder we have such a mess," he said holding the document up like he was scolding a junior engineer for cheating on his statistics.

Her stare back at him could have etched glass. "What do you want to do, Mr. President?" she asked with a tone that would have meant he was in the doghouse, if he didn't have a four year 'get out of the doghouse free card.'

"I want to," he paused for a moment and put the document back on the pile on the table outside the oval office. "I am going to take a few moments to make some calls. Excuse me. Hadid?" he said glancing at his trusted agent and dismissing Margery to go back to her calendar making. "I will be back in one hour," he said as he walked through the oval office doorway being held open by Hadid.

Once he heard the door click behind them, Riker began to speak. "Hadid, I need to..." Hadid had interrupted him with a hand up saying stop. He pointed up, made a sign that someone was listening, and motioned for him to follow. Riker moved quietly, as though tip toeing on the plush carpet would make it quieter. "find a good cigar in this town. Would you give me a few moments to look one up?" he said in a deception of his own.

Hadid held his magnetic card up to a wainscot panel in the oval office. It thumped softly and cracked open to swing into the room. He ducked under the chair rail as did Riker, and they entered a passageway. Hadid secured the door behind them and they walked for a few yards to a small seating area with six soft chairs and a small round table in the center. 'Who knows where this leads from here?' he thought.

Hadid motioned for him to sit and began speaking, "Mr. President, we need to go to Camp David as soon as possible."

"Why? Why Camp David?"

"The team you have requested will arrive there soon. They had a slight detour to Gulfport, Mississippi to pick up a young boy," explained Hadid.

"Why? Who is he?" asked Riker.

"Besides being the son of a very close friend, he is in mortal danger for what he has seen. He witnessed the event that let us know that the prophesy has begun to unfold," Hadid said in a very measured tone. "They will arrive within two hours.

"Two hours. Why can't they come here?" asked Riker trying to figure things out in his mind.

"There is a special secure complex there. Once we are inside, we will be safe."

"What do you mean 'safe'?" asked Riker. "This is the safest 10 acres on Earth."

"Mr. President, there are ancient forces at work here, that are responsible for that endless battle you were talking about this morning. We are here to stop them." He said.

"Stop them from doing what?" asked Riker, almost not wanting to know.

"Stop them from taking what does not belong to them."

"Like what?"

"Every soul on this planet," said Hadid. "Summon Marine One and let us go to Camp David. John and Enoch will join us on the lawn. We have to move now, Mr. President."

They stood up and walked back to the panel, opened it from the inside and walked into the oval office. Once the panel was secure, Riker opened the outer door and walked past Margery's desk. "I want Marine One on the lawn in 30 minutes, Margery. Can you make that happen?" said Riker dryly. He had to establish himself as the alpha male sometime in this term.

"Yes, Mr. President," she said, realizing that she had been given some marching orders.

He walked with long strides, but not to look like rushing. He was focused now on reaching his private quarters. Hadid matched his stride as they could feel the somewhat stale air of the White House on their faces. He needed a couple of things. He had the feeling he wasn't coming back any time soon.

Chapter 23

General Daniel D. Cabarrus was a mediocre officer. He was promoted mostly because he was a West Point Graduate and because he never made mistakes. He just wasn't brilliant, which made him the perfect high-level recruit for one the oldest and most nefarious leagues of henchmen the world has ever known. They were trusted by the elected leaders of their countries, but they ultimately answered to a being that had existed on the Earth since before the Flood of Noah.

There were originally 200 of them that arrived to watch over the young race of humans as they started out populating the planet known as Earth. There would be complications, because there were two races of humans, and then there were two tribes with the second race. The first race, known as lower Adam, was tasked to multiply and replenish the planet. The previous races had destroyed themselves and there were none that remained alive. They were created as males with genetically compatible females as farmers, mostly. They ended up domesticating animals as well.

The second race was made of descendants of Eve, with one tribe coming from Lucifer and one tribe coming from Adam. The watchers were supposed to guard the races and help them progress as needed. Lucifer convinced them to share their vast knowledge with his seed, and the race of man began to wage wars against one another. It would have been a short conquest, except that Lucifer convinced them to share of their knowledge with the greedy and lustful leaders of both sides equally. When one side gained the advantage, the slightly more advanced weapon was granted to the weaker side.

When the Creator discovered what they were doing, he revoked their travel privileges and doomed them to Earth with the very savages they were tasked with caring for. This is exactly what Lucifer had counted on, as it was precisely what had occurred on other worlds that he had visited. The watchers rebelled and began breeding with the females, both higher and lower, as well as animals. The results were so horrendous that the Creator had to kill everything with the exception of pairs of properly genetic animals and humans. If it had been allowed to continue much longer, there would have been no clean genetics left on the entire world.

Over the centuries, the watchers were imprisoned one way or another, by righteous men. A few were able to avoid capture and used their crafts and wisdom to work behind the scenes to feed the greed and lust for power of men and women. Humans had a very short lifespan, compared to any of the Nephilim, which was a blessing and a disadvantage for humans. Having the long range perspective is fine, but it tends to facilitate procrastination. The fact that humans proliferate very quickly made it easy to underestimate their ability to adapt and recover. It was all too easy to overpowered by a few thousand humans and end up in chains far beneath the surface of the Earth, or at the bottom of the sea. It was for precisely this reason that the Nephilim made use of men who sought after power to serve them in exchange for a little super-natural advantage. It was a little condescending, but men like General Cabarrus were all too easy to enlist.

"Hand me the secure phone, Major" said General Cabarrus to his aide, Major James Canfield.
"Here you are, sir"
The general took out a small notepad he kept in his inside breast pocket and looked up a number. He dialed it so rarely that it was not committed to memory. In fact, something kept him from memorizing it. "I am informed that he's stepping off the reservation," he said into the phone.
"He's called for Marine One. He's going to Camp David," said the voice on the other end. "Homeland Security

will trigger the Emergency Alert System and begin notifying people of the national emergency. Martial law will be implemented. You must be prepared to enforce it. We need the fear to be real. Understand?" said the voice with a well known authority.

"I understand," said Cabarrus. "What do I do with Riker?"

"He is assembling a team. They can stop us. Wait until they arrive at Camp David and kill them all. There will be no press. Make the jet look like it crashed. Do not fail me."

"Have I ever?" The line went silent. General Cabarrus turned off the phone and handed it back to the Major. "Contact the Rapid Deployment Team. We're at Camp David in one hour. We need martial law support and we need to neutralize the team at Camp David before they reach site R."

There is an access point near the Camp to enter the Raven Rock Mountain Complex, also known as Site R. It is connected to the Pentagon by a 97-mile tunnel. It has full Command and Control capabilities with accommodations for thousands. Once inside, the president would be inaccessible. It was virtually impossible to penetrate Site R.

The Major opened his tablet and began typing an encrypted message. O-P-E-R-A-T-I-O-N H-O-M-E-R-U-N 1400 hrs. He pressed send. He then typed in a message to the RDT. O-P-E-R-A-T-I-O-N S-N-A-K-E-B-I-T-E 1400 hrs Camp David. He pressed send.

This was a special tablet that had direct, encrypted access to a DHS fusion center network accessible only to the appointed leader of that facility. A well-rehearsed and extremely well-funded set of events were set in motion to take place at 2PM Eastern time.

The Major opened the sliding window accessing the driver's space. "The general's helipad, right now soldier." The olive green Ford took a right turn and accelerated.

"Major? Can I count on you?" asked the general.
"Yes sir," said Major Canfield.

Chapter 24

In 1950, President Harry S. Truman approved the construction of a deep underground facility that could be used as a relocation site for the Pentagon in times of national emergency. One half million cubic yards of superhard greenstone granite rock was secretly blasted out and hauled away in ten months. Five separate 3-story buildings were built deep inside the Raven Rock mountain located on the Pennsylvania-Maryland border.

The buildings look like ordinary office buildings set inside a hollowed-out cavern deep inside the mountain. The underground complex has roads and parking areas big enough to accommodate trucks and buses. Site R is completely self-sufficient with two power plants to generate electricity; multiple underground water reservoirs; and a sophisticated ventilation system. The facility can operate for at least 30 days in a "buttoned-up" position and can accommodate 3,000 persons in an emergency.

In addition to the basic life support requirements of power, water, and air, the underground metropolis also contains a medical and dental clinic, fire department, post office, dining facility, snack bar, dormitories, chapel, barbershop, fitness center, bowling alley, and even a Starbucks.

Marine One is a modified Sikorsky UH-60 Sea King designed to carry four passengers. It also has numerous defensive features and communications upgrades to sustain what the best think tanks surmised might be methods a terrorist might use to shoot it down. It can land in water and has deployable air bags to keep it stable in fairly choppy seas.

Riker walked briskly out of the White House with John and Enoch one step behind. He waved to the tourists and onlookers who happened to be in the area. He found himself practicing his wave in the mirror, because he didn't want to look like Forrest Gump waving to Lieutenant Dan as he jumped off his shrimp boat. This was an unceremonial trip, so there were no cameramen trying to catch him tripping or picking his nose. He snapped his salute to the Marine standing at attention at the bottom of the stairs.

Within a minute or two, they were airborne and heading for Camp David. "We will arrive before the team," began John explaining the mission. "Hadid left an hour ago in a smaller craft to do forward checks. He will have the vehicles ready when we arrive. You will take off again and remain airborne until we arrive at the entrance. We will draw any assault, because they won't expect you to be alone."

"Who would try to stop us?" asked Riker.

"We're not sure, but it is best not to take chances" said John. "You better put this on, Mr. President," said Enoch handing him a vest. "Your coat?" he asked as he held out his other hand. Riker removed his coat and put the vest on and velcroed the fasteners. Enoch stood to slide a hanger through the jacket and hung it up in the small closet. He removed a blue jacket with the letters FBI in yellow across the back. "Put this on," he said.

"FBI, huh? Clever," said Riker as he put his arms into the jacket.

"Resources," said Enoch. "A moment of indecision could save your life."

"I have a question," said Riker looking at Enoch. "It's been on my mind ever since that first meeting."

"I will answer if I am capable, Mr. President."

"How many of you are there? I mean, you say there is this ancient order, and they are scattered throughout the inner circles of the world's leaders. How do you all know what to do and when?"

"We do not serve two masters, if that is what you mean. We would not be allowed near the leaders, if we did not protect them with our lives and prove our loyalty to a certain extent," explained Enoch.

"I think he's asking about this mission," added John. "We do not have much time, Mr. President, so let me see if I can help."

"Of course. I wasn't implying that.."

"Quite alright, Mr. President. If I may," said John holding out his hand with the palm up as if to give something invisible to him.

"Go ahead. I just want to know," trailed off Riker.

"The dark prince has mighty men of old here on the Earth called Watchers. We are not sure how many there are, but we are fairly sure that the one called Semyaza is somewhere in this country and has infiltrated your military," began John.

"How can that be?"

"It is easier than you think. Men with this bloodline are lustful and full of greed. They are taught that their true inheritance was robbed from them, and that by using the dark secret combinations these ancient beings know they can gain back some of that wealth."

"Dark promises of great power and honor are delivered to them in this life, so their allegiance is easy to proffer in every age," added Enoch.

"Yes. Then comes the betrayal," said John. "It is a process of rules laid down before the worlds were created. It must be this way for the dark prince to claim victory."

"Victory? I talked about that very thing with the Joint Chiefs this morning. I was angry with them for conducting endless battles and never winning a war. No victory."

"Exactly, Mr. President," said John. "The plan is to addict the soul to violence and oppression, and preclude the mind to ideas like freedom and liberty. Once the soul has chosen to follow the dark path, he is prevented from seeing the light ever again, until it is too late."

"Too late for what?"

"Well, call it repentance. The redemption of the soul. The recognition of wrongdoing and a mighty change of heart," said Enoch.

"Oh. Guys this is really sounding a little like a Sunday school lesson."

"Then, let's call it resonance. If a soul resonates with the light, it will gravitate toward the light. If a soul resonates with darkness, it will have an allergic reaction to the light, and shrink into the shadows. Infinite degrees of shadows," said John.

"So I guess you're saying the whole world is doomed, because there is not much light out there that I can see."

"That is precisely why we are here on this mission, Mr. President, because that is not true," said Enoch.

"Yes," began John. "All over the world there are places where the light shines brightly. There are many more where the light has just ignited, and people are just now awakening. We have to get all of them to look and think in one direction on one frequency, so to speak."

"You mean like a second coming, or something," stated Riker.

"It doesn't work like that. Rules, remember? This planet is getting ready to separate into its two original parts. Like we do when we die. The difference is that we are talking about billions of souls that are alive and are free to choose which world is theirs," said John with tears nearly coming out of his eyes.

Enoch came to his rescue, as John wiped his eyes. "The dark prince wants to keep all those souls here on the temporal world. He believes that they are his inheritance, robbed from him in the Garden. His soldier is here, deep in a mountain, commanding forces inside our military, and he means to keep these souls from knowing there is a choice. Our mission is to provide that choice to them. Today," he said as he stood up in the helicopter.

"That's why we're going to Site R. The communications center," said Riker as he processed what they were telling him. He was a believer, but there was more than this. All his life, he had shown the ability to know when someone was telling the truth or not. Few people always told the truth. His wife did. He knew in his heart that these agents were telling him the truth.

They explained to him the message and the work that billions of souls around the world needed to do. They did not have much time. The Moon would be new in a little more than

117

24 hours. It was then that the Earth phases would separate and billions of souls would migrate to another place in the universe, while billions more would remain here with Semyaza and his captives. Well, not exactly captives, he reasoned. They would choose the wealth and trappings of mortality over the true inheritance that was promised in the Garden. Then, he had this wave of doubt come over him. It was like he suddenly remembered that he was here, aboard Marine One, heading for Camp David, a respite for presidents. He was the president.

"Oh Jesus," he said out loud.

"What is it? Mr. President," asked John.

"Why me? How can I..?"

"You are here for the same reason we are here," said Enoch. "Our Order learned about a prophecy that a leader will come from outside the conclave of evil. He will be chosen by the people in a remarkable, almost impossible manner, and he will be the one to say the message to the world. That is you, Robert Riker."

"But, I don't feel worthy to do this. I haven't done great things with my life."

"Feeling you are not worthy is one of the qualifications as well. And, you are about to do greater things than we have ever done," said John.

"We are 10 minutes from the motor pool," came the message over the intercom.

"You'll do fine, Mr. President. We will be with you," said John.

The helicopter was at tree top level now, traveling at more than 150 miles an hour. No radar could detect them at this altitude, and anything shoulder fired would have only a few milliseconds to aim and fire with the dense trees surrounding Camp David. The UH-60 was heavy, but it was in top running condition and the Marine pilot was the best in the HMX-1 fleet with more than 8 thousand hours in the air.

The craft banked hard to the left and swung the rear rotor around to slow down to nearly zero. The helicopter settled onto a parking lot next to a motor pool garage with 20 garage doors. John flipped the door open and dropped the air stairs. "We will call for you when we are ready. The pilot knows what to do," said Enoch. "Keep your seat belt on. It's going to be quite a ride."

The copilot emerged from the cockpit and grabbed the air stairs and pulled them in. He latched the door, turned and saluted the president, and then returned to his seat. Within seconds the Sikorsky leaped off the parking lot, and banked hard for the trees. It stayed low and the tail rose up high, while the main rotor chopped hard into the air like a leopard leaping for its prey.

He looked out the windows, but he could only see trees. They were actually flying close to the ground in clearings through the trees. They passed over a lake, and then a hay meadow, and then they dropped down onto a river and flew its gentle curves through the forest. Within a few minutes, they were deep into the wilderness surrounding the Camp.

Suddenly they pulled up and rose to the top of a mountain that was covered in dense trees. There were no roads. Not even a fire road could be seen. The helicopter circled and climbed higher and higher until the summit passed under them. Then, like a mighty bird of prey spreading its wings, it came to a soft landing on a flat stony area barely large enough for two helicopters. He could see out of the windows and just through the trees, but it was clear that this was a safe place that no one could see from any place except space.

"This is where we wait, Mr. President," said the pilot over the intercom.

Chapter 25

"We're 100 miles out from the airstrip," said the pilot over the cabin intercom. "Please stow everything and make sure your seat belt is fastened."

The team was tired still as they each woke up from their two-hour nap. Kyle folded his laptop closed and slipped it into the pouch of the seat in from of him. Orphan was sitting near the rear of the cabin, as he was the sixth member of the team.

"Can you tell me a little more about what you saw?" asked Loretta.

"I was standing on the highest tower of the rig, the Deepwater, with my roommate. It was nearly dawn and the view from up there is amazing. We could see the horizon, just barely, and these two waves passed by. They were huge, like two humps of seawater traveling, I don't know, about 100 miles an hour. The whole rig tilted back and forth and the casing failed. The gas pressure burst by the Blowout preventers and caught fire. The explosions destroyed the rig and killed 11 men. I escaped. My roommate was killed," he explained in the short version.

"The waves. Were they close together?" she probed further.

"Well, yeah, I suppose. They were like travelling together. I don't know how far apart they were, but they were about 100 feet high," he said using his hands to show the distance. "The first one kicked the rig one way, and the second one kicked it the other way."

"Which way were they going?"

"That was what was so weird. The sea was calm and quiet. There was no wind at all. Like black glass out there. And this is deep water, more than a mile. These waves were headed Southeast, I would say. Nothing can make deep water surge like that," he explained with all the authority a 19 year old oil rig worker could muster.

"Well, nothing except a gravity wave coming from inside the planet," said Rhino cutting into the conversation. "I did the math models. The two planets begin to emit harmonic waves of tremendous power. The model predicts that they will show up in the oceans first."

"What does he mean by 'first'," Kyle asked Dick. "I mean, 'first' seems to say that there might be a 'second.'"

"I think that is what he means, dude," said Dick. "What do you say doc?"

"Well," began Loretta." My hypothesis is that somewhere around the third full moon of 2016, that's the way the cyclic calendar works it out, the two earths are scheduled to begin their dissonance," she said flatly, hoping she didn't have to speak for a full semester to bring this crowd up to speed.

"That's like Easter," said Dick.

"More like Passover," said Kyle. "Ask a Jewish boy about phases of the moon and see what you get," he said waving his hand like a circle.

"You guys are closer than you know," said Bett finally joining in. "The Precession is a full cycle of star alignments that last for about 26 thousand years. I did the astronomical alignment calculations for Dr. Wesson's thesis." Up until now, she thought, she had been nothing but a conspiracy theorist trying to expose Smith and Jones. Everyone except Orphan had seen her bad side. She felt it was time they got to see how valuable she was to the team as a grad student.

"You might want to save this for the President," said Smith. "He has your thesis, but there are assumptions that are not explained," he said pointing toward the rear cargo area. "His team needs that information back there to be able to do their job."

"And what might that be?" asked Bett. "What exactly is their job?" she asked with renewed suspicion. "I have read for years about government contingency plans with your underground bases and special lists for certain elites that get admission while the rest of us get fried up here on the surface." She sounded like she was just getting wound up.

"Okay, hold it," said Loretta. "We've been through a lot the last 24 hours. We've seen a lot. I think they all have expended nearly superhuman efforts to see that we make it to this meeting, and they sound like they really need to know what we know. Let's try to show a little respect, here," she said with all the leadership she could muster.

"Okay," said Bett as she slid back in her seat away from the fight she had tried to start.

Smith turned around to face the cabin. "We will be landing soon. You need to know that we are not out of the woods yet. We need to reach the Camp David access door to Site R. It is located about a mile from the airstrip. Our team members will be there to help us. Make sure we leave nothing behind. All those records and things in the back have to make it as well," said Smith.

"We are on approach and have clearance to land," said the pilot over the intercom.

The jet began slowing as the pilot reduced the throttle. The flaps began to grab the cool, moist air typical with a Spring day in Maryland. Formally known as the Naval Support Facility, it has been the favorite retreat for presidents since Roosevelt. President Obama preferred the warm, tropical beaches of Hawaii and hated Camp David.

The landing gear doors opened and the wheels whined their way into position. There was no turbulence to speak of as the pilot lined up the jet with the long and wide airstrip. Since 1943, the facility had received hundreds of millions in black budget money to build the Raven Rock Mountain Center that was EMP and missile proof. It was deep under the hills with blast doors and a system of ventilation and accommodations to preserve the command and control during Cold War conditions and beyond.

The jet touched down and immediately began slowing and turning toward the side of the runway. The jet didn't taxi all the way to the tarmac to General Aviation.

"Smith, you better get up here," said the pilot over the intercom.

Smith quickly unfastened his belt and leaped into the cockpit door way, grabbing the door jamb to steady himself. "Are we going to GA?" asked the pilot.

"Good question." Smith held his wrist up to his mouth and spoke into his watch. "Let's hope he's in range. Hadid."

"We're on your 3 o'clock," came the reply over the watch's speaker Smith pointed to two white vans that were approaching the runway by driving on the taxiway. The pilot stood harder on the brakes and made the turn down the taxiway connector and off the runway.

"That's them," said Smith.

"Okay then, who are those guys?" said the copilot pointing to the other side of the runway near the end. There were four vehicles in desert paint approaching the far end of the runway about a mile away.

"I make that to be two troop carriers and two Humvees with 50's on top," said Smith.

"I gather they're not part of the welcoming party," said the pilot.

"Can you get us back in the air?" asked Smith and quickly he shouted, "Jones, we got problems!"

"I see 'em," yelled Jones from the cabin, leaning now against the front port window of the jet.

"Can't get up from here. I need more runway."

"Then go that way," said Smith, pointing to the forest about 300 yards away.

"Let me out. I can't do you any good in here," said Jones pulling on the door handle and cranking it over.

"We're turning," said the Pilot standing on the right pedal and applying the left motor. "You're going to have to close that door!" shouted the pilot over the screaming jet engine. Everyone in the cabin covered their ears and Jones dived out the door and rolled to his feet outside beyond the tip of the wing. Smith grabbed the door and pulled on it.

Rhino jumped out of his seat and grabbed the door next to Smith and pulled it closed. "I got it, sir," he said.

"Hey buddy, do you think you can you pick up anything?" Dick said to Kramer.

"Good question," said Kyle opening his laptop and waiting for it to boot up.

Jones could be seen running toward the two vans as Hadid opened the back of first van. They were pulling a trunk out onto the ground and opening the lid.

"We have to move," said Smith to the Pilot. Take us toward the woods over there. We need cover and to get out of this plane."

"Hey there is nothing on the air from these guys. They ain't saying anything over the radio," popped Kyle as his scanning program was running. "Lemme try something else."

"What about fuel management. Those are diesels," said Dick.

"Yeah hold on," said Kyle as he furiously dragged and tapped his finger around the touchpad.

"Go go. Punch it," said Smith slapping the shoulder of the pilot.

"I can go, but we might not be able to stop once we leave this pavement," he answered as he gripped the yoke in anticipation of the rougher surface. A small jet has a small tiller crank by the left of the pilot and the right of the copilot. "You're going to have to help me with this."

"I am ready to follow your lead," said the copilot. There is no feedback to the operator. The tiller simply directs the hydraulic pressure of the nose wheel steering gear. It takes practice, even with a stripe to follow on the pavement. Too much lateral pressure will snap the strut loose from the airframe.

"Let's stay out of the tall grass. There could be soft places that will bury the nose wheel."

"Got it," said the copilot.

"What do we have in the case?" asked Jones sliding up to Hadid with his slick dress shoes on the pavement. He didn't realize how fast he was running, but the incursion force at the end of the runway would be within range in less than 2 minutes.

"I have an M-60 with a mix of phosphorus and Depleted Uranium rounds," said Hadid.

"Damn. That's heavy enough for hard work."

"You're going to have to hold it. We don't have time to mount it," said Hadid.

The second van was chasing the jet and almost caught up with it. John was at the wheel and Enoch was sitting in the passenger seat. "They're heading for the trees," said John.

"Pull up to the pilot's side. He can't see us. I will get him to stop," said Enoch.

John floored the van, and it bounced with the off-road conditions and spun a cloud of dirt up behind the van. Enoch rolled his window down and waved his arm to get the pilot's attention.

"Hey Smith!" yelled Rhino. "There's a van next to us."

"Oh. That's good. That's good. Stop the plane right here," said Smith putting his hand back on the pilot's shoulder. The pilot stood on the brakes and the plane lurched in the hard dirt to a stop. "Everyone in the van right now. Go go go."

Rhino snapped the door handle open and flung the air stair down. He jumped down the stairs and ran back to the cargo area behind the wing. The port engine was still winding down and making an awful noise. Loretta and Bett were next down the stairs and ran for the open side door of the van. John grabbed their hands and helped them into the van and onto their seats.

Rhino arrived at the back of the van with three boxes. "There's more," said Rhino to Enoch who turned to run with Rhino to return to the plane.

"Let's go guys," said the pilot to Dick and Kyle who were huddled around his laptop screen.

"Go on. We just have to do something. You won't leave us. Right?" said Dick.

"You have just a few seconds," said the copilot as the next one to pass them.

"Come on, guys. We must go now," said Smith. "They will be here is less than a minute, and it won't be pretty."

"It will be more than a minute," said Kyle waiting for the hack to complete its task. "I just shut their fuel pumps off. Now we can go."

Dick stood up with Kyle right behind him and they jumped down the stairs of the jet and ran up to the door of the van. Within seconds they were in their seats. Rhino and Enoch had the last of the boxes from the cargo area and ran for the van.

At that moment there was a whizzing sound as rounds began flying past them in the grass. Jones lowered his eye behind the M-60 and returned fire from first van just to let the approaching forces know they were not unarmed. "You guys go on. We'll hold them here," yelled Jones.

"No need. Their vehicles are down. Fuel systems," said Smith pointing to Kyle who grinned and held up his laptop. "Let's go."

"Rhino, can you give me a hand?" yelled Jones from the other van.

"You da man, Jones," he said favoring his weak leg to get over to the first van.

"These windows tilt out, but they're bullet proof. Can you remove this one?"

Rhino unlatched the passenger side back glass of the van door, swinging the bottom of it out. His massive hands wrapped around the glass and snapped it free from the upper hinge. He tossed it away into the grass. "Like this?"

"You are the man, my friend," said Jones. "Get in." Jones tossed the M-60 machine gun into the van next to the ammo can with the belts, hopped in, and closed the van door behind him. He stuck the M-60 out of the back door glass and yelled to Hadid, "Drive, Hadid! Stay close behind them!"

The two vans drove down the curvy road through the woods. It was meant to be a training ground for Navy personnel, but it was repurposed into a rural retreat for presidents and their families. The smooth asphalt roads were made for golf carts or horses for them to enjoy the beautifully groomed forest land that was preserved with the camp. For security reasons, the roads were never mapped on paper. Only those who had actually been to the camp knew where the roads went, and how they connected to one another. It was easy to get lost, but not so hard to walk out of the woods if you stayed on the roads and followed the blue arrows in the middle of the road leading out. Right now, they were driving against the arrows.

"Where are we going?" yelled Jones up to Hadid.

"We're following John. He knows the way," yelled Hadid over his shoulder.

"People call me Rhino," said Rhino holding out his right hand as he climbed into the passenger front seat of the van.

"Agent Yafil Al Hadid. People call me Hadid," he answered releasing right hand from the wheel. It means,"

"Iron rod," said Rhino.

"Actually iron bar, but that sounds okay" said Hadid. "Do you speak Farsi?"

"Samoan," he said pointing to himself. "I played football with people who did. That's where I heard the name before."

Hadid smiled. This man was easy to like. His heart felt good.

"Is the president here?"

"He is coming in on Marine One. We will meet him at the access door."

"Way cool." Rhino was excited about meeting the president. He was 26 years old, but only voted in one election. This one. He wrote in Robert Riker's name along with 50 million other people. It was his way of sticking it to the man.

"Do you guys know where you're going?" Bett asked Smith.

"I know where it is located," said John. Smith did not answer her. He looked straight ahead. He changed. Shots had been fired, which meant their mission had been compromised. These were not terrorists, he reasoned. These were federal troops. They knew the jet held precious cargo and where it would land, even though no one in their group had communicated with anyone outside. They had changed their flight plans in route, been to the edge of space, and flown with a dark transponder. There was no one on Earth that could have tracked them.

"Crap," he said softly.

"I know," said Enoch. "It's him."

Chapter 26

"We are on stealth approach," said the Army pilot of general Cabarrus' helicopter.

"Major. Radio silence. Got it?" barked the general.

"Yes sir," said Major Canfield. He sometimes felt like a junior lieutenant the way the general ordered him around. He was a commanding officer from Fort Bragg when the expansion happened at a cost of more than $180 million. North Carolina loved it, but the sequester debacle crippled the military structure during the Obama administration. Cabarrus and 15 other generals were relocated from the Pentagon to Fort Bragg. Canfield was transferred to staff duty during the merger.

Like a giant corporation, many seasoned professionals were fired or transferred to streamline the operation and reduce costs. The result was a loss in command flexibility. Everything became micromanaged. There was a fever of competition as generals lusted after one more star. Cabarrus ended up on the Joint Chiefs because he was the last man to step back. No one wanted the job with Obama. His disdain for the military was expressed on a weekly basis as he refused to attend meetings. He would send his staff to listen and take notes, and then he asked for briefings to be sent to his tablet in bullet points.

Twenty-one generals took early retirement rather than sit in that circle jerk of a meeting week after week. Cabarrus took the job, thinking it would give him another star. The sad commentary was that it did. His gruff and opinionated manner was annoying, but for some reason he was favored in nearly every respect. Someone up there really liked him.

Major Canfield was a good soldier and wanted to make colonel more than anything. He was promised that rank for his loyalty. He was not alone. The president's pressure on the military created an atmosphere of lust for power through favors and bribery. Most admirals and generals fought the sequester and Obama's targeting of the American people while supporting the Muslim Brotherhood. They resented Muslims with ties to terrorist groups serving in the Administration. Some of them spoke out and were summarily fired with severe gag order penalties placed upon them. No books. No public statements.

Hundreds of captains and colonels also retired early, forfeiting their military careers rather than serve under such leadership. Canfield was tempted, but the chance to reach the rank of colonel brought with it an enormous raise in pay, and once he reached that rank, he could not be riffed. He could retire with 75% of his base pay for the rest of his life. So, while the others were jumping ship, Major James Canfield was being promoted. It felt good. But sometimes, like right now, it felt bad enough to jump out of this helicopter without a chute.

"Major!" shouted the general.

He snapped out of his pensive state of mind. "Yes sir."

"You kick some ass with these troops when we land. I am expecting results." He said boring into him with those dark eyes.

"Yes sir." The general did not like talk about what you were going to do. 'Results,' he would say. But, if you started talking about details, he would say, 'I hear a lot of cluckin', but I don't see any eggs.'

The helicopter swooped lower, once it cleared the trees of Camp David near the Eastern edge of the runway. With an eastern breeze, they knew the jet would land from the west, over two miles away. There was no line of sight visibility to the staging point, just inside the trees.

The Major jumped up as the Black Hawk landed firmly and shut off its engines. He slid the door open and hopped to the ground, putting on his helmet. He walked briskly over to the two open troop carriers and heard the sergeant yell, "Attention!" There were two Humvees with gun emplacements on the roof.

This was a good platoon, although there were no rangers in the group. These were hand-picked warfighters with close combat experience. They looked like mercenaries to him. They had short beards, tattoos, and did not wear the uniform correctly, he thought. They were picked because they would take orders; any orders.

He stared at the men one by one, loosely in line, each one holding his weapon on a tether up close to their chest with their right hand wrapped around the grip and the index finger extended over the trigger guard. Well, trained, he thought. The general approached from behind and to the right. He did not speak, which was rare for him. Instead he turned and walked toward the first Humvee, opened the passenger front door and climbed in, slamming the door. The Major could tell he was looking through the bullet proof glass at him, watching his style.

"At ease," he said. The men shifted their stance to something less than attention. Military bearing was not their strong suit. "In a few minutes a jet will land at the other end of this runway. There is a small group of insurgents on board with stolen classified information they mean to expose. We are not going to let that happen."

"Sir, no sir!" they said with a shout that surprised him. They didn't look the part, he thought, but these 16 men have fought as a unit before.

"There is a man with them who resembles the president. Do not be fooled. This man is an imposter and has a mission to seize control of the Site R communication center. We will stop him from achieving that mission. Am I clear?"

"Sir, yes sir!" they recited.

"When that jet touches down, and not before, we will contact and destroy it on the runway. No survivors. Everything burns. Acknowledge!" he spat.

"Sir, yes sir!"

"Radio silence. We let the Humvees lead and the troop carriers flank either side when the plane is stopped."

"Sir, we have chatter. They have clearance to land. They are wheels down," said the pilot as he emerged from the helicopter.

"You stay here and in the chopper," pointed Canfield. "Let's load up. Wait for my lead in the other Humvee." He opened the passenger front door and slid inside, closing the 100 pound door behind him.

The Sergeant Major barked his orders, "You heard him. Load up and secure for engagement." Seven men piled into each of the two troop carriers and pulled the ramp door closed. The other two men climbed aboard the Humvees and assumed positions behind the swivel gun emplacements.

The turbocharged 5.9 liter Cummins diesel motors growled to an idle with a small puff of black smoke out of the vertical exhaust stacks. The two Humvees had exactly the same motor with the VP44 fuel injection pump system. These motors had incredible torque, capable of towing just about anything, but they had one excellent feature that high performance enthusiasts valued. They had a small, electronic control board that could be externally reprogrammed.

"There it is," said Major Canfield to his driver. "On my command, let's head up the runway. He waited for the plane to disappear behind the rise of the runway. "Okay, let's go."

The Humvee surged forward as the turbo spun up. The gearing produced a top speed of only 70 miles an hour, but the troop carriers could do barely more than 55. The carriers split up with one taking the far right side of the wide runway, and the other hugging the far left. The Humvees stayed side by side and took the center of the runway. In just about one minute, they would have the plane in sight.

The Major looked out his side window at the other vehicle. The general was staring straight ahead. It was in the hands of Major James Canfield now. It was his command. He could feel his moment approaching. He rolled down his window so he could feel the wind in his face. He felt exhilarated. He had been sitting at a desk for ten years, filling out supply chain and administrative paperwork. Every "I" was dotted and every "T" was crossed. One by one the other captains had been attrited. He chuckled quietly. That word, coined by General Norman Schwartzkoff during the first Gulf war. His television briefings to the American people were like high stakes sports programs where enemies were "attrited," instead of blown away or killed by precision smart bombs. He was the last captain, and he was promoted to the rank of Major. Soon, very soon now, he would be promoted again.

"Corporal, I think we need to go faster," said the Major realizing that they were slowing down. "I can see the jet now, driver. We need to go left. Let's go," shouted the major."

"I've got it floored, Major," whined the young driver. "I'm turning. I think we're all stalling out, Major."

Sure enough, the major looked to the right, and the general could be seen pounding the dashboard. He was sure there was a similar conversation going on over there. He looked to the left, where a troop carrier should be flanking the white jet that had suddenly braked and turned completely off the runway into the dirt. That truck was also as slow as they were going. "Are we all out of gas?" he shouted at the corporal.

"No sir. We have a half tank. The throttle is not responding. We are at an idle," shouted the corporal.

"Gunner, do you have a target?" the Major yelled back at the mercenary gripping the 50-caliber machine gun.

"They're a mile away, sir, but I can maybe hit the jet or those vans over there," responded the gunner.

"The other vehicles are waiting for my signal. Fire a burst. Shoot them!" he yelled.

The gunner squeezed the hand triggers and the gun chugged a dozen rounds shot in the direction of the jet, now shrouded in a cloud of red dust from something. Within seconds a short burst of 30-caliber rounds came back toward them. One round went neatly through the skull of Major James Canfield, and broke the femur of the gunner. The driver, his face splattered with the Major's blood and bone fragments, stopped the Humvee in the middle of the runway.

He punched his seat belt and opened his door, exiting the vehicle onto the runway. He vomited while wiping the blood out of his eyes. No more shots were fired. There was a new commander now.

The general ordered his Humvee to stop as well. He opened his door and stood up on the door sill while holding onto the grip handle in the doorway. He raised his other hand and pointed his finger up. He waved it in a circle. The troop carriers stopped as well, and the rear doors opened. The soldiers poured out and began running toward the general's Humvee.

As they arrived, they were clearly out of breath. It was nearly a 100 yard dash for all of them. "They're escaping through the woods on the trail roads. There is an access door to Site R back there," he said pointing to the north of the runway. "They have about 3 miles to drive. We are about a mile south of that access door. You two," he said pointing to two youngest and tallest of the soldiers," get to the chopper back there and tell them to come and get us. No radios. Got it?"

"Yes sir," they both said as they instantly began sprinting back the way they had come.

The UH-60 Black Hawk can carry 20 lightly equipped troops. They had 19 left, with the unfortunate demise of Major Canfield. Light arms would be all that is needed in the close quarters of the stone hallways inside Raven Mountain. The two runners arrived at the helicopter, still running as fast as they could. It reminded them of combat training.

The copilot met the approaching soldiers in the open side door. "Just you two?" asked the copilot.

"Sir, the general would like you to relocate to pick them up. We are 12 o'clock on the runway about a half mile out," said one of the troops.

"Welcome aboard," said the co-pilot stepping back to the cockpit. The door stayed open as the pilot began spooling up the twin General Electric T700-GE-401C turboshaft engines. Within less than a minute, they were lifting off and tilted toward the general's position. It took slightly more than a minute to travel the half mile, because they had to accelerate, climb out, and negotiate the landing on concrete. 17 more troops entered the helicopter in remarkably good order and sat on the floor close together.

"Take us to the "A" access portal of Site R," yelled the general.

"Yes sir," said the copilot. "Hold on. We're heavy."

The Black Hawk spooled up loudly and lifted slowly off the ground. It leaned slightly and went forward, still well within the rated payload. Within seconds, they were traveling 100 miles an hour and heading for the parking area near the access door. Raven Mountain had been connected to Camp David with a tunnel that was 6.2 miles long. Camp David is 90% wooded area with a few clearings and erosion control areas. Beneath the forest floor is almost solid green granite for more than two thousand feet, making the area nearly impervious to attack. Within 3 minutes, the copilot turned around to face the general.

"Sir, we will land on the helipad across the street. Without radio contact, I do not know if the access door is open or even manned."

"You let me worry about that," said the general.

The Black Hawk sunk to a landing on the helipad at Site R, and the doors slid open. The troops and their commander exited quickly. "Lock and load, troops," shouted the general over the din of the twin engines. "Sergeant Major, take 8 soldiers into Access Door A across the street from here," he growled. "It goes back in about 100 yards and connects to Access door B. Position yourselves in the main hallway, and you can cover both entrances. You see something, kill it and call me on secure channel 2," he said handing him a radio. He twirled his hand over his head and hopped back in the helicopter with the 7 remaining soldiers to leave the area. It spooled up and lifted off. "Take us to Access door C," yelled the General to the pilot.

Within seconds the Black Hawk lifted off and headed east toward Access door C. The facility is built like a giant right triangle with a pair of access doors at each base of the shape. Along one of the legs was the air and water processing stations. Along the other was a complex of 6 buildings built into the ground down to 950 feet deep in the green granite. They were flying across the densely wooded mountain along what would have been the hypotenuse of the triangular structure. They were low across the trees to keep their noise to a minimum.

When they touched down at Access door C, they opened the doors and jumped out onto the paved area. The general twirled his finger again, and the helicopter spooled up and within seconds had disappeared over the trees, heading back for the airstrip. "Let's go. We will stop them from entering the complex by holding this access hallway. No prisoners," he said flatly.

Chapter 27

John was making steady progress on the trail roads through the forests of Camp David. They were paved perhaps 30 years ago, and the condition had deteriorated, especially during the 8 years Obama was president. Normally, funds from the federal highway fund were carved out for maintenance of the largely wilderness area. Snow and ice took their toll, but fallen branches and leaves from the hardwoods and small rock slides were a constant source of maintenance for the preserve. Rhino and Orphan got out several times to pull large branches or rocks to the side, so they could get through.

"We're getting close now," said John. "The access door opens to a large hallway that is about six miles long. That leads to a domestic water supply area that branches off to the main hallway leading to the Communications Center in building E."

"I haven't seen any sign of those guys in the Humvees," said Dick. "Kyle, are you picking up anything on your receiver?"

"There is a HAM signal and some FM stuff coming from the North, but I assume that is the business at Raven Rock," he said tapping on his touchpad.

"There's a clearing up ahead," said Smith into his wrist watch. "Stop just short of that, and let us do some scouting."

"Roger," came the reply from Jones. The vans slowed and stopped, while Jones and Smith jumped out. Smith ran up to the front van. "I think we need to call in the president," said Jones as Smith approached.

"I don't like it. It's a sniper's paradise here," whispered Smith.

"You really think they'll try to take us here? With all this surveillance and civilians?"

Smith motioned for John to come out and talk to them, then pointed to Hadid in the rear van. John opened the driver's door and shuttled around the front of the van to meet them. His tall frame moved with the flexibility that decades mastering martial arts will produce as he buttoned his center coat button. Hadid slid out of the driver's seat and came around the other side.

"We need to call POTUS and have him join us," said Smith. "We think they will try to stop us inside the facility, but we're not sure where. What do we have in the way of weapons?"

"I have my Glock and this," said Hadid producing a narrow curved blade that had the look of ancient origin.

"That's pretty close quarter," said Smith. "Anything else?

"There's the M-60 in the back and some short rifles in the combat case," said Jones.

"That's more like it," said Smith.

"Where do you think they will be? Given the troop carriers we fired on, there could be 15 or 20 of them," said Jones.

John squatted down to the ground and picked up a small twig on the ground. The parking area near the vans was flat and sandy. "Here are the four access doors," he said drawing the layout of Site R in the sand. "Two here, and two over here. The two A and B hallways are about 300 yards long until they curve together to one main hallway. That hallway is about 500 yards long, passes by the underground reservoir and reaches the power plant here. Go past the power plant and you reach Building E. That is our destination. The Communications Center is on the 3rd floor. There is a blast door. Once we're in there, no one can stop us."

"Now, the other entrances are C and D, located way over here on the East side. They also have 300 yard long hallways, but they connect to a main hallway about a half mile long. It turns right at the domestic water supply pump station. We go past the east power plant and start at Building A. We have to go through the shopping areas that makes up the ground floor of the first four buildings to get to building E."

"The Camp David access door right over here," he pointed with the stick down the road they had driven earlier, "has a 6 mile hallway, but it connects a quarter mile behind the connector for access doors C and D. It is brand new and known only to secret service, because this is the president's access. Only our cards will open it." John was the only one of the team that had seen this tunnel.

"I don't suppose we have any night vision," asked Jones.

"Wouldn't do any good in there," said John shaking his head. "It's a cave, remember? If we kill the lights, it will be completely black."

"I think we they will try to stop us at the access halls of the west and east entrances. We should be able to get behind them and into the communications center without being detected," said John.

Enoch approached them from behind. He was at least six inches taller than Smith. Standing between them, he placed one of his enormous hands on Smith's shoulder and one on Jones's shoulder. "You did fine work, my brothers. Did you see the phases?" he asked in his deep voice.

"We did," said Smith, nodding slightly.

"We were weightless up there," said Jones.

"It is time we bring in the President and share all Dr. Wesson's findings. We should retreat into the woods and find respite until darkness. Our adversary is expecting us now." He paused for few seconds, "Let doubt become our ally, not our enemy." And with that he squeezed the shoulders of the two men firmly and smiled.

"Where is the nearest clearing?" asked Smith with renewed confidence in his direction.

"There is a vehicle storage building in a clearing about 4 hundred yards south of the east power plant. It is about 2 miles through the woods this way," said John pointing to the rear of the front van.

"Okay, let's go. When we get there, flash the coordinates to Marine One," said Smith.

With that the five men divided up to their vans and they headed down the trail road toward the clearing.

"Where are we going now?' asked Loretta.

"To a clearing not far away. The president will meet us there," said Smith.

"Those guys back there shot at us," said Dick. "Why?

"The information that Dr. Wesson has is vital to national security. There are some that do not want this information to be known," said Smith.

"Each of you has been called together for this team for a reason," said John. "Each of your abilities is part of this plan."

"I don't mean to bust your balloon, there agent John, but it doesn't seem to me like any of you have a plan. This planet is coming apart at the seams, and there is no plan that I can see," said Bett.

No one spoke for several seconds while the discomfort of what Bett had said sunk in. They were without a clear direction. They were innocent participants, each of whom connected the team better than they knew. The Sun cast long shadows by the time their vans made it to the small clearing around the maintenance vehicle shop. The parking lot was empty, and the garage doors were closed. Tall, evergreen trees surrounded the small amount of asphalt and the block building with a silver metal roof. Smith texted the coordinates to Marine One and he waited for an acknowledgment. Within seconds, his phone vibrated with the response. "They will be here in a few minutes.

"The president? He's coming here?" asked Rhino.

"Stay inside until the helicopter is gone," said Smith.
"There will be loose gravel and sticks kicked up."

Kyle had fallen asleep on the bench seat behind them with his laptop on his chest. The van load was quiet. Every life had changed in recent days. Some had looked forward to this day with endless hours of study and calculations. Some had been told stories since their youth in preparation for events for which they would play crucial roles. Some had supplied key technologies that delivered the entire mission to this point in safety.

One, however, was a witness. To him had been given the first sign that the end of the age had arrived. His heart was tender at this moment, and for the first time in his life, he wished he was somewhere else. "Smith?" came the quiet inquiry from Orphan.

"How are you doing, son?" asked Smith as he moved from the front bench of the van back to where he was sitting. Standing, he held out his hand to shake his hand.

Orphan responded by extending his hand, but the grip was weak and vacant. "Can I call my dad?" he asked with the little boy reaching out of him.

"Sure. Here you go," Said Smith as he handed him his cell phone. "We have a few minutes until the president arrives. Go outside, if you need to."

"Thanks." Orphan opened the side door of the van and stepped out onto the gravel parking lot.

He dialed the private number and waited for the answer. "Dad?"

"You made it? Hadid got you?

"He sent two secret service agents, Smith and Jones. We're at Camp David waiting to meet the president."

"Riker? He's a good man. Are you alright?" Abdulla perhaps expected Orphan to grow up too fast. He knew there would be terrible trials for this boy. His own past would haunt him, but there he knew Orphan was wiser than his years. He had known from dreams that this son was being saved for a special purpose. He was important to God.

"Well, yes. But I miss you. I miss mom."

"I know. We will be together soon."

"Well, that's maybe why I'm calling. They say the planet is coming apart. It's dying. I don't know what to do."

"The ancient records speak of this," he said in Farsi. "Earth may pass away, but our souls will live forever. We never lose each other." The words sounded so poetic in this language. But was he sure?

"But dad, I saw it. I saw the waves. They lied. We lost 11 men on that rig, and they lied."

"I know. The top people knew when the sign would occur, and they moved their money. I know everything. But you don't need to worry about that. You stay close to Hadid. His father saved my life two times. We have a tradition," he said with the best encouragement he could muster. He was a faithful man, but he had sinned as well and wondered if God would grant him one last prayer.

"Dad?"

"Yes, son."

"I love you."

"You are more than water in the desert to me," said his father in Farsi. So poetic.

"I will see you soon?"

"Yes, son. I promise."

This time he got to connect to his dad. There were no games. There were no hard words to be brave or to never let down his guard. All of those years of discipline and challenge were to prepare him for this. He felt peaceful. He felt loved. What more could any man want in his life, he thought. He walked back to the van, where Smith was waiting outside the door.

"Are you okay?

"Yeah. It's all good," he said. He handed the phone back to Smith. Smith put his hand on Orphan's shoulder and looked into his eyes. No longer able to hold it back, Orphan wrapped his arms around the neck of Smith and buried his face in his shoulder. Pausing only for a second, he returned the embrace and patted him firmly on the back to let him know everything was strong. He was done. He took a deep breath and released Smith. They nodded to eachother and Orphan climbed back into the van.

Smith took a deep breath and flexed his powerful shoulders into the warm spring sunshine. The worst was yet to come, he thought. Just then, he heard the quiet and distant thumping sound of Marine One and it suddenly came in across the tree tops and leaned back for a short landing. He squinted and moved behind the van until the rotors had quit cutting the air. He ran to the helicopter just as the air stairs were coming down. The president was standing at the top of the stairs. He quickly came shuffling down to shake Smith's hand. He looked up and saw John, Enoch, and Jones standing in front of two white vans next to a small block building. They walked quickly to the vans, shook hands and the agents turned their backs to the helicopter, shielding the president, as Marine One powered back up and disappeared over the trees. Within seconds, they could hear nothing but the sounds of Spring with birds chirping in the trees around them.

"Are you thirsty, Mr. President?" asked Hadid.
"Yes, a little. You have some scotch?"
"Sorry, Mr. President. Red or blue?" asked Jones as he held up bottles of Poweraid.
"Red is fine. Is this my team?" he said cracking a bottle open and taking a sip.
"And then some, said Smith. Hadid, will you introduce everyone."
"This is Dr. Loretta Wesson," said Hadid.
"Ah yes. You're the one with the thesis full of clues," he said shaking her hand.
"And these are my grad students. This is Bett Dyson."
Bett stepped forward with her manly handshake and said, "Nice to meet you Mr. President.
"And this young man is Rhino. He's the.."

"The Rhino? Not the running back, Rhino."

"Yes sir. That would be me. Rhino at your service, Mr. President."

"And these two men save our lives in California. Richard Daring is a famous racecar driver," he said pointing to Dick. "And this his engineer, and might I say an extraordinary genius and handy to have around," said Hadid.

"Mr. President," they each said shaking Riker's hand.

"This young man is a special charge of mine. He was there when the first waves came through," said Hadid with great respect.

"The witness. Nice to meet you," said Riker.

"Orphan Bayazed, "he said with a nod and a handshake.

"Wait. Bayazed. Isn't he the owner of the LA Times?

"Yes sir. That is my father."

"You know I would probably not be president without him?'

"Really?" said Orphan with a smile on his face.

"Really. Don't tell anyone, but he ran all my ads for a dollar. Something about that man," said Riker holding his index finger up.

"My friends, we have a mission at hand, and the hour is drawing near," said Enoch from behind them all. He always seemed to know the right thing to say at the right time.

"Yes, well. Where do we start?" asked Riker.

Chapter 28

"They won't be expecting us to slip in behind them in this tunnel," said John pointing again to the map he had made in the sandy part of the parking area. "We'll be at least a quarter mile behind them, if they are stationed here at the junction of these two entrances and the main hallway."

"That makes sense to me," said Smith.

"What do you think their rules are," asked Jones.

The agents looked at one another and were silent for a moment. If these were mercenaries, they would follow orders and shoot to kill. If they were soldiers, they might not fire on agents or the president. It was hard to tell.

"You need a scout," said Orphan. Again he opened his mouth before he knew it. "I'm just saying. I was a receiver on the football team. If I go by myself, they might think I work there. I could check it out, you know ahead of the rest. They're looking for a group, like us, right?" he asked.

"You are not taking a risk," said Hadid. "You are my responsibility, and I will not allow it."

"It's what your father did for mine," said Orphan.

"I can't believe we're even doing this," said Bett. "You can't let a boy walk into that place and get himself killed."

"She's right," said Smith.

"You don't patronize me. We wouldn't even be here if it wasn't for you," she screamed as she stepped forward and slapped Smith across the face. She wanted to punch him, but she got her point across.

Smith barely blinked, and he did not raise a hand or change his tone in the slightest. "You go. You take the point position," he said coldly. "Take my watch and walk ahead of us to each corner. They would never expect you by yourself," he added.

"Okay I will," she spat as she grabbed Smith's watch.

The group was nervous and embarrassed for the energy of that exchange. Smith took one step toward her, calmly. His powerful hand took her left hand and gently turned her arm over as he took the watch from her. He looked into her eyes. "You will be safe," he said smoothly. "Count your steps. Every 40 steps speak into this part here," and he lifted her wrist now with the watch fastened in place. "Each time you say 'clear' we will stay 40 steps behind you." He paused for a moment and lowered her hand. Bett was almost in a trance of calmness as he released her. He looked at Enoch and nodded gently.

"Get in the front van," Smith said pointing to the five civilians. "The rest of you on me at the back of the other van." Rhino held the door open for them as they each jumped into the van and found a seat. As Bett passed him, he leaned in close and said softly, "You da man."

Smith opened the back door of the van, and Hadid grabbed the combat case and opened the lid. Inside were 4 short rifles with folding stocks and four clips loaded with rounds. There were also 4 semiautomatic pistols, which he handed out to the agents. Jones grabbed up the M-60, but Hadid placed his hand on top of it. "We won't need this in there," he cautioned. Jones, almost with a look of disappointment, withdrew his hand and took the pistol and put it behind his back inside his belt. He accepted the short rifle as well.

"Our mission is to make sure the president reaches the communications center. It would be very nice if everyone else made it without injury," he said looking at the front van.

"Understood," said Jones. John, Hadid, and Enoch nodded as well.

"Enoch, are you alright with that?" asked Smith as he looked at the black pistol in his hand.

"It will be put to good use," he said as he placed the gun behind the front of his belt.

John took the left side to take the driver's seat. The others moved up the right to slide in tightly next to the others already in the van. The door closed, and the van started up. "Take us to the access door," said Smith. They were quiet as the van weaved along the trail road through the dense forest. In about 5 minutes, the road became much darker as the trees were close together and very tall, blocking the early evening light even more. They came around a bend, and the road forked. They took the left side and in a hundred yards, the road was blocked with an iron pipe painted red and white. In the center was a white metal sign with the words "Trespassing beyond this point prohibited by the United States Secret Service."

"That's us," said Jones. He hopped out and raised the pipe on its weighted hinge to allow the van to pass. He lowered it behind the van and returned to his seat.

"Just like Area 51," said Kyle quietly.

The van continued along the road that looked much newer than what they had been driving all day. They passed four, almost brand new gray job trailers parked on the side of the road on a perfectly paved miniature parking lot. There were no vehicles parked in front of them, and there were no lights on inside our out. After a few minutes they came to a dark recess in the cliff wall. John stopped the van. "This is it."

"Doesn't look like much," said Kyle.

"I think that's the idea," said Dick.

"Whispers only, team," said Smith. "The sound will carry, even though you won't be able to make out words once you're 10 feet apart. Really bad acoustics in there."

John approached the door and took out his magnetic card. He held it up near the small red LED that was illuminated on a smooth black panel. There was a noticeable clunking sound, and the door opened outward. The entire team moved inside quickly, as John used his card to close the door behind them. It was dark, with the exception of small yellow lights along the two side walls near the floor. It was an optical illusion, but the two rows seemed to go forward into the blackness of space, meeting far out in front of them.

"Hey, look at this," said Kyle who had wandered into a side alcove to their right. He took out his cell phone and tapped it, illuminating the room. He walked up to a wall switch and flipped it up. Soft lights came on in the room, which was occupied by 2 small golf carts and 4 large electric golf carts with three bench seats. Two benches faced forward, and one faced backward. They were all plugged into brand new receptacles. Kyle twisted the key on one of the carts, and the green light came on. "They're fully charged."

"Looks like we don't have to walk six miles. We ride," said Dick as he pointed at Kyle using his right hand as a six shooter.

"This makes it easier to be quiet and fast," said Smith. "Bett, you take the first cart and ride out in front. Act like you work here. We will follow in 2 carts behind you about 100 feet."

"I'll go with her," said Loretta. Smith began to object, but she held up her hand. "Who is going to expect a couple of girls in a golf cart?" Smith exhaled in frustration, glanced at Enoch, and waited. Enoch nodded almost imperceptibly.

"Okay. Jones, we'll take the front of the second cart. Hadid take the rear. John and Enoch the front of the second, and Rhino on the rear. Mr. President, you take the center seat behind them. You two are with me."

Within a minute, they were lined up in the narrow hallway with Bett and Loretta in the lead. "Let's head out. Go until the dead end. It is 6 miles that way," said Jones over his wrist watch. The carts started out slowly, trying to gage their distance. Within a minute they were racing silently along at 15 miles an hour. The tunnel air was cool but surprisingly clean smelling, the results of a state of the art ventilation system making air capable of sustaining 3,000 people deep inside Raven Rock Mountain.

After twenty minutes at full throttle, the visual effect was quite mesmerizing. The two LED paths merged far ahead in the darkness to a single point, and yet the yellow lights passed them on either side mile after mile. It was a breathtaking accomplishment to realize that so much granite had been carved out and removed, leaving a smooth and flat floor beneath their golf carts. "Clear," said Bett into her wrist watch. She wondered for a moment if Smith was going to let her keep the watch.

"I see something," said Loretta almost whispering.
Bett was pulled from her trance and let off the golf cart accelerator. There was a faint orange glow from the horizon far ahead of them. The cart slowed instantly and she reapplied the throttle to approach the glow more slowly. The yellow lights were spreading now, but still she could not see much further than the orange glow ahead. Then, she realized that she was not looking far down the road. She was looking into a dead end of a much higher wall ahead of her.

"It's another road," said Loretta.
"Oh yeah, I can see it now."
"Stop stop stop," she said. Within a few seconds, the other carts had inched up behind her.
"It's the main hall," said John. "We should go left. We'll reach the domestic water supply and pump house and then around that to Building A."
"Is there anyone in the hall?" asked Jones over his wrist watch.
"Hold on. I'll see," said Bett. She got out of the golf cart and walked up to the intersection. The hall was wide, perhaps 40 feet, and the ceiling was about 25 feet high. She could see for a long way down each direction, but only the soft, orange glow of the high-pressure sodium lights could be seen. There was no sound. "Nothing either way," said Bett quietly into her watch.
"Okay, we go left. Same speed as before. About a third of a mile to go and bear left around the pump house.

We're going to stay further back, but we have you covered," said Jones.

The carts began moving again. "I think we got behind them," said Jones to Smith.

"It looks like it," answered Smith as he drove the cart and strained his eyes to look ahead of Bett's cart.

Within 5 minutes, they swerved smoothly around the pump house. There were a few staffers walking along the road on the right side behind the fat white line that formed a pedestrian zone. They never looked up at the carts going by. It all looked and sounded normal.

They came up to a large sign that said Building A on the right side. The bright yellow bollards protected the large glass double doors that indicated the entrance. Within a minute, they reached the sign that said Building B. Within 5 minutes, they were coming up on Building E. Bett stopped her cart by rushing up to the bollards and jumping out. She knew they were close, and that nothing had happened so far. She was nearly in shock after holding her attention so sharp for so long, thinking at any moment she was going to be shot at. She and Loretta jerked open the glass doors and stepped inside the lower lobby area of Building E.

Within seconds, the others were right behind them. "Great job," said Smith.

"The elevators," said John. "Third floor."

"They're down there," said Rhino pointing the way and hobbling ahead.

The five agents formed a shield around the president now, with four tightly behind him and Smith in front. They moved smoothly toward the elevator. "Stand away from the elevator," said Smith to the others. To the sides. More. Okay, press the call button."

Four short rifles were aimed at that door when it opened, but there was only a woman holding a purse inside. She let out a short shriek, but was relieved when she saw the five dark suits and the blue jacket. Still, she exited the elevator and shuffled with her high heels toward the exit on the other side of the lobby.

"We all go," said Smith. All ten people moved into the elevator with the civilians in the back, and the president kept in the middle of his secret service team. The door closed quietly. "Press three," said Smith.

"Get ready," said Jones. Each man slipped his finger inside the trigger guard of his rifle. Their eyes were ready for a target. As though being crushed in a compacter, they felt the pressure of time as the moment for the doors to open approached.

The door opened, and there was no one outside the elevator. The agents went out with the president and scanned the room, including behind the unoccupied furniture in the small third floor lobby. Ahead of them were two, steel doors with a sign that said COMMUNICATIONS CENTER.

"We're here," said Smith.

The elevator doors began to slide shut behind them. "Hold that door," said Kyle. He slid across the floor, holding his laptop up so it would not get damaged. The doors closed against his shoulders, as he lay on the floor to make sure they would not close. Slowly, he got to his feet, holding one in the doorway as he reached the number pad. "Four, five, six, two and one," he said punching the buttons. "What? Just in case they are behind us, they will have to wait a long time for the elevator," he said smiling.

"Nice one, buddy," said Dick.

"Jones, on me," said Smith as he shuffled forward to the doors while looking through his combat sight. Jones grabbed the door on the right, twisted the handle and jerked it open while Smith marched forward inside. He turned around, and raised his rifle. It was clear. The rest of them hurried inside the doors. "Take the president to the mike. You know what to do," he said pointing to John. "The rest of us will hold here. See if that door can be locked somehow."

"I think there are mag locks on the doors," said Kyle. "See these pads? They're magnets. In case of fire they release to close the doors and remain unlocked to let people out."

"Then how come they aren't locked?" said Dick as he pulled open the door.

"Hmm. Let me check and see," said Kyle as he sat down on one of the orange, curved chairs like you would see at a dentist's office lobby.

"Here it is Mr. President," said John.

"You're sure about this?" he asked. "People out there are actually going to know what I am talking about?"

"Yes, sir. They will know. They have been prepared for many years," said John.

At that moment, Enoch walked through the single door into the radio room, where the president was now seated at the microphone. John was about to initiate the Emergency Alert System, when he looked up and saw Enoch's raised hand indicating to wait a moment. "You must clear your mind of doubt, Mr. President. We have told you all there is to know, but this is no time for faith. That is for those who hope for things unseen. We are beyond that into the region of consciousness called knowledge. Speak the truth of the universe, for we are escorting a planet through its own transition of death into a new life. It is why we are here. It is why you are here." He opened the door and stepped out into the hallway and the door closed quietly behind him. At that moment, John raised the clear shield over the red, mushroom head button marked EAS. He pressed it.

"Whoah!" said Rhino with a jump.

"What was that?" asked Dick.

"The doors. The mag locks. They engaged," said Kyle.

"What did you do?" asked Dick.

"Nothing. I didn't even get into the system yet. The security system requires biometrics," said Kyle.

"Jones, I can't get this door open," Smith said as he tried to open the radio room door.

"It's the security protocol. He's on his own in there now," said Smith.

"He's got John," said Hadid. "We hold them here," he said as he drew is blade and tossed it from one hand to the other.

"Keep trying to see what you can do," Smith said to Kyle. Bett, you and Loretta get down that hallway around the corner. Orphan, I'm counting on you to keep them safe. Go on. Jones, you and Hadid take my sides. Rhino?"

"I got your back, sir," said Rhino.

"You do not. You're a civilian. Get over there behind that couch," ordered Smith. He moved to the side of the room opposite the couch and chair thinking that whoever was coming through that door would shoot through it first. "Enoch? You. You."

"I'm with them," he said calmly as he walked over and sat in the chair behind which Dick and Kyle were kneeling, shaking."

"Those magnets will hold quite a bit," said Kyle. "But with enough force, they can be pulled open."

The room was so quiet, they could hear the air moving through the cold air return in the drop ceiling.

"They're coming," said Enoch.

Chapter 29

"Sergeant Major?" called General Cabarrus with his cell phone. "It's been four hours. We have seen nothing of them."

"Same here, General," responded the Sergeant Major.

"Let me put together a scouting party. We'll see where they are," growled Cabarrus. He ended the call and rubbed his stubbly beard with his other hand. At that moment, his phone vibrated in his hand. It was NORAD. "Cabarrus," he said shortly into the phone.

"The EAS has been activated," said the deep voice on the other end of the phone. The Nephilim leader was deliberate and clear.

"We set up kill zones in the two access halls in front of the building complex," he said.

"They have gained access another way," said the voice.

"We are only a few hundred yards from there, but my other team is over a mile away through the tunnels. It will take time to get."

"We do not have time. They will change everything. Go now and kill them all."

And with that the General recoiled from the force of the darkness on the other end. He ended the call and immediately redialed the phone. "They have got behind us. They are already at the communications center," said the General.

"Nothing has slipped past us except some grocery delivery folks, but there were only three men," said the Sergeant Major.

"There must be another tunnel I don't know about. Get to Building E third floor as quickly as possible. We'll be there in less than 15 minutes to back you up, but do not hesitate to engage. Repeat, engage them immediately upon arrival. Double time, Sergeant Major," he shot into the phone as he ended the call and slipped the phone into his pocket.

"We go to Building E right now. They have initiated the EAS. Weapons hot. The other team will be engaged when we arrive, so look alert. Let's move out!" shouted the General.

They headed down the long main hallway at a jogging pace. He knew the Sergeant Major would arrive first and at least contain the area, if the president's team was well armed. He also knew they had a number of civilians with them, which would not be a problem to eliminate.

Jogging for a mile in the cool tunnel as a combat team was at first fortifying to his resolve. He had a mission. He always accomplished his mission. But then, he started to think about the task of assassinating a sitting president and what that meant to the government he swore to defend.

His team did not know that this was the real president. He had told them he was an imposter, and that his companions had stolen classified information. But these were not newly enlisted ground pounders. These were not recruits. They were seasoned mercenary types with multiple tours in hostile territories. They had never fired a round in the US, and certainly had never put an American citizen in their gun sights before. He wondered if his leadership was enough. Would they follow his orders?

He recalled a story of Viet Nam, when American soldiers had taken a Red Cross team into a remote village to inoculate the people against small pox and malaria. When they returned to the village two weeks later to use it as a staging area for assaults against a North Vietnamese weapons depot, they were shocked at what they found. In the center of town was a pile of severed arms.

Only the arm that was used to administer the inoculation was cut off, and they were stacked in the center of town. It was not a lesson of horror of how vicious the enemy they were facing might be. Far from it. It was a statement of respect for how perfect the North Vietnamese soldier was for following such an order. Did he have perfect soldiers? Was he the perfect leader? Was the dark power that used his lust for power and rank powerful enough to command these men to follow him, no matter what? He lowered his head and breathed deeper while he jogged in front of his troop, in an effort to strengthen his will to follow his master.

The eight men who jogged beside and behind the general were of one mind, strangely enough. They had seen battle before, but never like this. It seemed like they drank pure adrenalin for days on end cleaning out the small, disorganized streets of Bagdad, Takrit, and the endless maze of Fallujah during the surge. They followed a lieutenant or a warrant officer, but never a general. Their efforts barely got them a pat on the back. If they got hurt, the medical system was focused only on the process of getting their warfighter back into the field. They felt like plow horses at times, turning over the dirt of the Middle East, so something else could be planted in its place. They each believed that this mission, for which they were hand-picked, would be close to the top of the food chain. There would be promotions. There might be bonuses. They knew the truth was not important, because at the end of the day, they were never there anyway.

They were making good time, and they could soon see the domestic water supply pump house. It was running, but there was no one outside the structure. The musky smell of water and plastic is slightly more difficult to breathe as smoothly as they had done for the previous mile. They pushed on past the door that said Building A. The sweat dripped from their faces and they could tell their shirts were soaked. The cool, cave air made the green cotton of their camouflaged fatigues cold against the skin. It was a different environment than the sweltering dry heat of Iraq.

156

Building E came quickly, and the team split up between the stairs and elevator. They would enter the third floor during a fire fight, because the sergeant major's team would already be engaged. The team had already depersonalized the combatants they were about to face. It would be easy to end them all, no matter what they looked like. They had heard the pleas for mercy a thousand times. You squeezed the trigger and watched them die anyway, knowing that the innocent would be sorted from the terrorist by the creator who gave them life. The General had given them orders. It wasn't their prerogative to question them. No military force could survive if the soldiers continually questioned the orders.

There was blood splattered on the stainless steel walls of the elevator and a half dozen small bullet holes in the rear wall when the General and four men climbed inside. It was okay. They knew the Sergeant Major was as tough as they come, and he would have charged anyway. There would fewer to fight when they arrived. The enemy would not expect a backup force.

The door slid shut and the elevator surged for the third floor. When the door opened, they would shoot everything that was not in fatigues. Within seconds of their arrival, the other four soldiers would burst through the stair access door, creating a cross fire that would confuse the enemy and make them feel like their situation was hopeless.

In the few seconds before the elevator reached the third floor, they might hear gunfire and men screaming positions and handoffs. They might hear a woman's scream. And then the elevator came to a stop. In one or two seconds, the door would open, and there would be nowhere to hide. There would be no choice but to run forward into the fight. There was no beachhead. There were barricades. Only the drawbridge of the elevator doors opening into the fray would deliver them into the chaos.

But there was no sound. There was no gunfire. The doors opened, and the room was dark as night. They could smell the cordite of battle, but only the elevator door light illuminated the room. Within seconds they rolled out of the door and scattered around the room. They were standing at first, with their eyes straining to see something behind their backlit reticules. There was nothing. A chair. A couch and some small tables. One, three, seven bodies lying on the floor in camouflage in the lobby area. One pair of booted legs could be seen a few yards away lying in the hallway, the body just out of sight around the corner.

As though like a sudden collision, the other 4 men came tumbling through the stair access door. The General jumped in his skin and almost fired his drawn forty-five semi-automatic pistol at the intrusion. As though frozen in time, the eight men stood there gripping their rifles and moving their red dots around the room to try to find a target.

Battle was always confusing, and it almost never went exactly the way it was planned. Something was always out of place. "This room is secure," whispered the General. "Let's go down that hallway. Follow me." The general had always seemed to have a guardian angel around him. He could walk through a battle with bullets whizzing all around and never seem to get struck. He told his former wife that he had special powers, and that nothing could hurt him. She left him after one of his particularly violent drinking binges where he stood on top of the coffee table with his forty-five and yelled at the demon to come and get him.

The men pointed their semi-automatic combat rifles down the hallway, and the General began to move. Suddenly, there was a flash of sound. Rhino was still behind the couch where Smith had told him to be. As the blast of guns and the sound of orders and the grunts of bodies being struck with bullets, he remained secure. Now it was time to move.

Rhino put his shoulder against the couch and pushed as though he was crashing through San Francisco's defensive line. The couch struck the 8 men standing behind the general and took them off their feet. At that same moment, the lights in the lobby came on, there stood Jones and John with their rifles looking down at the pile of soldiers on the floor. They were quickly disarmed. "On your bellies, snakes," yelled Jones. "hands on the back of the head."

The general was missed by the couch and ran down the hall. Rhino stood up and began to move after him. As if in slow motion, they moved down the hall, the side door opened and Smith came into the hallway from the radio room. Riker was close behind him. That was his mission. It was time to complete it. "Riker. Time to punch the clock on your presidency you phony bastard," he growled.

Bett moved before Loretta and Orphan could stop her. They were huddled at the end of the hallway behind a large potted plant. "Put the gun down, you son of a bitch," she yelled with her fists bunched up tightly.
"My mother used to say the same thing. You think I won't should a woman, if that is what you are? Think again," as he raised his forty-five caliber semi-automatic pistol in line Bett's approaching body and squeezed the trigger.

As though the bullet came out of the four and one half inch barrel in slow motion, it twisted through the air at eight hundred feet per second and stopped upon entering the chest of agent Michael Smith. He had leaped in front of the shot and saved the life of Bett Dyson.

"No!" screamed Bett as she unclenched her fists and tried to reach for the fallen agent. It was too late. Riker grabbed her a few moments later and pulled her into the radio room and slammed the door. The General swung his gun toward the door the same second and began pulling the trigger over and over again. Each round punched through the insulated steel door, leaving a hole the size of the average thumb.

Bett had fallen to the floor with her hands over her ears in a rage of tears and grief. The bullets flew over her head and struck the opposite wall beside the radio console. The raging General moved the gun with each shot in an attempt to cover the distance across the room with his maniacal mission to assassinate the president. Four, five, six the rounds kept coming.

As though in one fluid series of events, Rhino's enormous fist smashed into the general's left cheekbone, shattering it and driving him to the floor of the hallway, very close to the still warm body of agent Smith. "You are not da man," said Rhino.

As the shooting stopped, Riker opened the door, now pocked with holes, he emerged to face John.

"Mr. president, we must complete the message to the world. We are running out of time," said John

"But agent Smith is down. He needs..," Riker began.

"That's his job, Mr. President. Let us take care of him."

Enoch returned from the front room where Jones and Hadid had the eight soldiers held on the floor at gunpoint. He walked over to Smith and looked down at his motionless body bleeding onto the tile floor. He picked up the General's gun still clutched in his hand and handed it to John. "Go on. Take the president inside and continue the broadcast," said Enoch in his deep resonant voice.

President Robert Riker turned his back on the hallway and walked back to the radio console. John gently closed the door, sealing Bett's exhausted sobbing inside the radio room as though to disconnect her from the body of agent Smith.

Chapter 30

"This is president Robert Riker of the United States of America. To the Americans hearing this emergency broadcast, I don't know if you voted for me or even if you know the sound of my voice. I am reaching you as well as the global community through a series of translation computers here at our secure headquarters at the Emergency Alert System.

"April 10th, just a few days ago, the Deepwater Horizon exploded and caused the largest oil spill in history. It was a tragedy, to be sure. But there were many who knew it was coming. Oh, perhaps not the exact day, but they knew that the third full moon of 2010 would signal the end of the age, and this would fulfill a prophecy spoken about for more than five thousand years.

"Here is what we know. Planet Earth is composed of two complete versions of Earth; one is very high frequency, and the other is low frequency. They were merged together nearly six thousand years ago, and have been rotating in relative harmony ever since. Until now.

"The two frequencies were predicted to become out of phase with one another. To make it simple, the higher frequency Earth is beginning to separate from the lower frequency Earth. Many of you already know this. You can feel it. But the majority of the humans alive on this world are trapped in a physical viewpoint of this mortal life.

"That is the way the low frequency or dark beings in this universe want it. They want you to stay asleep, or they want you choose violence or greed, or lust, fear or hatred. If you do not listen to and act right now on what I am saying, you will miss the transition this higher frequency Earth is about to make. I tell you that you were born here at this time to make that transition. It is your inheritance, if you choose to accept it.

"There is another heritage on this planet as well. It also has been here from the beginning, and it means to keep you in darkness and doubt. It wins when you decide to choose the accumulation of the material things of this world and to reject mercy and charity and love. It wins when you dig a pit for your neighbor. It wins when you participate in the harm or death of another life. It is important that you stop killing one another, including our unborn children.

"This dark and terrible heritage is driven by a raging jealousy of the people who have chosen the spiritual rather than the physical aspects of mortal life. The seed of Lucifer, descendants of the first son of Eve, are driven mad with their claim to the birthright of ownership of this planet. They seek to rob you of your inheritance and to doom you to an eternity of darkness. You see it all around you in terrorism, a religion of fear and death, and the constant mantra that there is no dream for you. They do not know what happiness is, because that gift is denied to the wicked. Oh, they know pleasure, and all its twisted levels, but they do not know joy. They don't want you to know it either.

"I want to, excuse me. There is a...I need to...I will be right back. Do not go away. Grab your family and friends, and I will be right back," said Riker. There was the sound of rapid gunfire, and the yelling of men, and crashing of things to the hard tile floor outside the radio room.

John threw open the door to come inside with Smith right behind him to protect the president. The instant he came inside, it seemed, General Cabarrus appeared behind him. Before anyone could move or respond, there was a loud report from the General's forty-five. The sound was deafening as the bullet left the barrel and entered the chest of agent Smith.

162

The rest of the events were a slow blur to Robert Riker. The door was slammed shut, and general began firing rounds at him through the door as he kept moving toward the side wall away from the series of shots. Just as it seemed he would run out of space to run, the gunfire stopped. It was quiet, but his ears were ringing, and the smell in the room was of burnt cordite. He opened the door slowly.

The general was down. Bett was seated on the floor inside the radio room deeply sobbing quietly into her hands with her back against the wall. He walked out of the door for a moment to check on Smith, said something, and was directed back to the microphone at the console. The message. The rest of humanity was waiting on the other end.

He sat down and turned the broadcast key to talk. "This separation will be cataclysmic, at least as cataclysmic as the joining of the two Earths during the Great Flood. Many of you may die. There are other ways through which you may die in the next few days and weeks. If you do what I ask you to do, it will not matter. The restoration of your spirit to your body will be seamless and painless, if you choose it to be.

"First, I need you to participate with me in this exercise. You must take a moment to sit calmly and focus on the good in yourself and in others. Develop a love for yourself and then expand to include other people, even people you do not know. You can call this prayer. You can call it meditation. It is all the same, because you will be led naturally to the same place. It does not matter at all which religion you come from, because the gateway is identical for all. One of the greatest deceptions of the dark prince was to create religions, and then to make each religion hate the other. These are all the philosophies of men, mingled with truth so that you will follow it. I am asking you tonight to realize that from here on out, all churches are dissolved into two kingdoms, one of light and one of darkness.

"Breathe in through your nose and out through your mouth for a few minutes. This will calm your body and focus your mind on my words. It will allow you to listen to the higher frequencies in my words. Try to do it sitting up, because if you lie down, you will fall asleep and then you may be unaware of the lesson that is pouring out right now over you. You must reach out to this energy first, and then it will envelope you in its power and protect you.

"A short time ago, we just completed an historic election in America. Now, I am reaching out to you for an historic election for the planet Earth. If you choose to do what I am asking you do to, you may still die here, but you will be reborn on a new world without death and violence. Still, many of you will choose the physical wealth of this world. For that choice, you will remain here on this world, but we will no longer be your victims. This is a sure election, and there is no one that will choose for you. Search your hearts right now, and you will know I speak the truth.

"As you extend your thoughts to the love I have been describing, you may become aware of another world in synch with this one. It is sort of like another dimension that you get to see. It is right here with us, but you must choose to see it and be with it. I am asking you to take that journey with me. Prove now, whom you will follow."

Enoch stepped up beside Riker as he pushed back from the microphone for a minute. He placed his warm hand on Riker's left shoulder and leaned down to meet him face to face. "You have placed things in motion, now, Mr. President. It is time to leave this place. But, before we do, there is something you must do."

"What more can I do?" asked Riker.
Enoch withdrew from his pocket a small, gold tablet. It was very thin, and it was very curious in its detail. It was

shiny and clean like it was brand new, but it had the feel of something that was older than the Earth itself. Enoch handed the relic, about the size of a small paperback book, to Riker.

"What do I do"? asked Riker.

"Place your right thumb in the small square in the lower right corner of the side with all the writing on it," said Enoch.

Riker held the strangely heavy tablet in both hands for moment and looked at it. Slowly he let it go with his right hand and placed his thumb onto the small square. The tablet vibrated slightly in his hands, like it was turning on or something. As he removed his thumb, the symbols on the surface of the tablet began to illuminate, as though they were backlit by some light within. A small, thin line of light began to form from the top center to the bottom. What do I do now?" asked Riker.

"Break it," instructed Enoch.

"Break it? Like snap it in two in the center?" asked Riker.

"Yes, Mr. President. Snap it into two pieces."

With that, Riker gripped the tablet in his two hands, and bent the stiff tablet between them. At first, it resisted, as though it was titanium and not pure gold. And then, suddenly without warning, the tablet snapped in two pieces. As that moment there was a shudder in the mountain complex like a soft explosion had taken place. The difference was that it had the feeling of pressure being released from something around them. The vibration continued for about one minute, and then it trailed off into silence.

"We must leave now, Mr. President," said Enoch quietly.

"Why? What did I just do?" asked Riker.

"That, Mr. President is what is known through the historical writings, as the sixth seal," said Enoch.

"It is written, 'And I beheld when he had opened the sixth seal, and, lo, there was a great earthquake; and the sun became black as sackcloth of hair, and the moon became as blood;

And the stars of the heavens fell unto the earth, even as a fig tree casteth her untimely figs, when she is shaken of a mighty wind. And the heavens departed as a scroll when it is rolled together; and every mountain and island were moved out of their places. And the kings of the earth, and the great men, and the rich men, and the chief captains, and the mighty men, and every bondman, and every free man, hid themselves in the dens and in the rocks of the mountains; And said to the mountains and rocks, Fall on us, and hide us from the face of him that sitteth on the throne, and from the wrath of the Lamb: For the great day of his wrath is come; and who shall be able to stand?'," recited Enoch.

"This is the process of the Union of the Polarity described by Dr. Wesson earlier today. Both of the Earths contribute a part of the mortal experience that humans enjoy on this planet. Some people are aware of the beautiful and pure things of the higher Earth. Some people only see the dust and weeds and death of the lower Earth. Over the past generation, these two types of people have become increasingly unaware of each other.

"In one observation, the human sees the endless variety of nature and the peaceful harmony of man within it. There is challenge and limitation, which the soul longs for more than anything else in the universe. There is room for exploration and discovery. There is room for new life and an abundance of love and really there is no need for the rule of law, because humans of this type spontaneously obey this higher law. To them, this world is the closest thing to heaven they can imagine.

"In the other observation, the Earth is here simply to conquer and consume. Humans with this heritage and propensity gain insatiable pleasure from causing the suffering of others. The hereditary drive they feel for destruction and oppression is as powerful as the desire to reproduce. Like their great ancestral father, Cain, they slay others and take what they have. They cannot dream of anything, they cannot produce anything except the opportunity to rape and murder and oppress the peaceful humans of this planet. They destroy everything they can find like the locusts described in history. They plague the Earth in a similar way, consuming every resource and every green thing in their path, if they are not stopped by good men.

"Well now, at the time of the fourth new Moon of this year, the Earth has shown us her readiness to deliver. The man who has been prepared, and chosen by the people, has explained to the world from one source at one time, the challenge of this time. And, he has now broken the sixth seal in accordance with the prophecy. Now, these things will come to pass, and the human race of this world will inherit what it will, either eternal light and goodness or outer darkness and the absence of innocent victims from which it gains its only pleasure," Enoch explained.

"Please, Mr. President. Let us go outside and see the dawning of a new day and a new age."
With that, the president handed the two pieces of the tablet back to Enoch and stood up to leave the radio room in which only the two of them and Bett remained. It seemed like it had been hours since the battle. Bett was exhausted and fragile as she stood to walk out with Riker's arm supporting her.

Enoch was behind them, as Riker opened the door into the hallway. They looked down at the floor, and there was nothing there. There was no body of agent Smith. There was no blood. The holes remained in the door, so they knew they had not imagined it. They walked down the hallway to the large cement pot behind which Orphan and Loretta hid for protection. They were not there. They walked back up the

167

hallway to the communications center lobby, and there were also no bodies and no blood. The chair and the couch were put back in place, but Rhino, Kyle, and Dick as well as the agents and soldiers were gone.

"Take the elevator down to the first floor and take the golf cart. Return to the Camp David access door," said Enoch.

"Agent Enoch, I will need you to come with us," said Riker.

"My path takes me elsewhere, Mr. President. The others will meet you outside the mountain complex at the access door at Camp David. I will see you at another time," said Enoch. They both knew it was true and inevitable. This tall, pale skinned man was calm and pure and seemed to possess knowledge, or at least a confidence, far beyond his young appearance. His blue eyes looked at both of them and seemed to say that they were going to be safe now. The elevator door closed quietly, separating them from Enoch and began its slow descent to the bottom floor of Building E.

There was a single golf cart parked outside the double glass doors of Building E. It was the same cart Bett and Loretta had used several hours before. Several days? Who knew? It was timeless in the oversized tunnels of Site R. There were no clocks that they could see in the complex, except for inside individual offices on the wall. The lighting remained unchanged year after year. Riker imagined what it would be like to escape a cataclysm down here, living with 3,000 other people. Would the human race go crazy? Would they all end up pale like Enoch and John? He helped Bett sit in the cart, and belted her in the passenger side.

"Where are they?" she asked in a distant and exhausted voice.

"I think they are outside the complex," he answered. "We're going now." He pressed on the accelerator, and the cart surged silently down the giant hallway toward the small

168

passage that led to the forest at Camp David. They were both silent until they made the turn down the passage lined with the yellow LED's.

"Do you really believe what you said to the people?" She asked.

"Well, I had never heard of it before just a few days ago. And, don't forget this morning, or yesterday, I don't know now when exactly it was. We've been down here for who knows how long? We went through all of Dr. Wesson's data, and yours, and Rhino's. The science is a big stretch for me, but there doesn't seem to be anything that sounds too outrageous. Considering what Orphan saw, and the evidence of the unwavering long term focus of evil in this world, I suppose I do believe it. I said it like I believe it," said Riker.

"I have been living life with my head for so long, it is hard for me to feel any more," she began. "I have protected myself from feeling, except for the rage I have against the machine of government and oppression. It's like they don't want us to do anything or think anything on our own, without their approval. You know what I mean?"

"More than you know. When I was started my campaign, all I came up against was this regulation, or this fee, or that law, or that rule that would not allow me to enter the race, even though I knew it was legal. It was unfair. Well, I guess the establishment's candidates took their play acting a little too seriously, and the name calling and mud smearing became so repulsive to so many people that millions of people wrote my name in the slot for president. Now, the whole world is coming apart, literally."

"Well, I am glad you got the job. I didn't vote at all. Now I wish I had, so my words would mean more. But I think you are the right man for the job. Hopefully, you can fix all this crap," she said as she took a deep cleansing breath.

"It isn't as easy as one might think. Hell, one of the joint Chiefs just tried to assassinate me. Do you think there is anyone in the government I can trust?"

"Yes I do. You can trust those guys in the suits. You could trust Hadid. You could trust," and her words were choked off by the sadness inside her, "Smith."

"Hey, hey. In some sense, Enoch was right. That was his job. That level of commitment to a government job is like nothing I have ever imagined. But those guys are a special group inside that special job title. They have a global order that puts them in front of every bullet aimed at every world leader. I get it now, but I didn't at first," he said. "He gave everything he had to this order."

"I doubted him. My last words to him were angry. I was confused and scared," she sobbed quietly as if to say these words too loudly would cause her to burst open in endless crying.

"I am sure he didn't take it personally, Bett."

"Well, for what it's worth I am making a change in my life. That's for sure. This hurts too badly."

"We're almost there. We'd better be getting there soon. This cart is beginning to lose some of its get up and go," he said lightly.

"If I remember, it is just a little further up ahead," she said trying to recover from her state of mind.

The cart rolled forward in the ethereal passageway with the yellow LED's relaxing both of them. Within a few minutes, the orange glow from the lights inside the cart charging room were visible up ahead. The cart slowed, and Riker turned into the room. All of the carts were parked there, except the one they were driving. "Well, that's reassuring. Everyone else is already here. Let's get out of here. Maybe we can find a good cup of coffee."

"Yeah. I mean yes, Mr. President."

"Bob. You can call me Bob as long as there aren't any cameras," he chuckled.

"Thanks for being so kind. I just,"

"That's no problem. I'm sure we still have a lot of work to do yet. Let's go."

Chapter 31

"How much damage can he do? I mean seriously, he is a nobody that got elected president," said General Wes Morlay. NORAD is an old community of defense contractors, career military personnel, and politicians. In the late 1950s, a plan was developed to construct a command and control center in a hardened facility as a Cold War defensive strategy against long-range Soviet bombers, ballistic missiles, and a nuclear attack.

The mountain was excavated under the supervision of the Army Corps of Engineers for the construction of the NORAD Combat Operations Center at Cheyenne Mountain beginning on May 18, 1961, by Utah Construction & Mining Company. The Space Defense Center and the Combat Operations Center achieved Full Operational Capability on February 6, 1967 at a total cost of $142.4 million. System Development Corporation was contracted to update Air Defense Command satellite information processing systems for $15,850,542 on January 19, 1973. Although software was barely a notable concept in 1973, the beginnings of the Internet were called the WATTS line, and computer screens were black with green text and drawings.

By 2008, the obsolescence of the hardware became undeniable to a political class that was less interested in warfighting superiority, when all the original functions of the complex were removed to Peterson Air Force Base. President Obama became more interested in funding social programs and initiated a poisonous policy of sequestration that gutted the expansion funding across the board for military programs. The old NORAD facility, secured under 2,000 feet of solid granite, became nothing more than a training and simulation facility, or so the public was led to believe.

Semyaza is a timeless being. He led a contingent of angels to Earth in the eons following the seeding of the planet by the Creator. 200 beings of immense wisdom and knowledge with experience from numerous worlds covering hundreds of thousands of years were assigned the task to watch over mankind. But the generations of mankind are very short, compared to a Nephilim. There were several things that were immediately evident, but there was one unique aspect of this creation that existed nowhere else they had been before.

Humans bred in the normal way. They coupled just like any mammal found anywhere in the universe. There was an instinctive urge to do this, and the gestation periods were less than a year, and the cranial capacity was nothing short of phenomenal compared to all other forms of life. They not only responded to stimulus, but they adapted in mere moments to different conditions and situations. They could show incredible fits of violence and rage, but these same beings could also exhibit compassion and love that was very close to that of the Creator.

What became apparent to them was that although the genetics of humans was programmed to grow old in a matter of moments, it seemed, the spirit inside of these bodies could gain experience and learn complex concepts, and then remember them from generation to generation. Not all souls learned as well as others. Some could pass away in the flesh and then, through shear desire return to inhabit another physical body. Some of these souls could retain their skills from mortality to mortality.

The Watchers became painfully aware of the importance of the Creator's claim that he had created higher Adam to be in their likeness. This was an ability that they would never have, thus they were given the ability to live almost forever. They gained wisdom and knowledge simply because they lived so long. They would not die for tens of thousands of years, and thus they could not reproduce between themselves. But what they learned while on the most fertile and beautiful worlds ever created almost ruined the entire creation.

At first, the Watchers were content with teaching certain individuals on Earth how to do things. They taught the women about makeup and that the power of beauty was so great, that if properly applied almost any man could be weakened and destroyed. They taught men how to make swords and arrows, scimitars and spears, canons and missiles. They taught men how to fight and even more importantly, they instilled in them reasons to fight.

They created churches and that it was impossible for man to approach God without going through one of them. Then, they taught the leadership of each church, that every other church was evil and inspired each one to proselytize all other churches. The confusion was nothing short of divine.

The Nephilim eventually became enamored with human women and helped develop them into the most beautiful creatures in the universe. Lucifer saw his chance to accomplish the greatest upset in all of existence. He awakened desire in the Watchers. His offspring, through the blood of his union with Eve in the Garden of Eden, was seeking dominance over the entire human race. But Adam's seed had been given the inheritance of the planet, and were blessed in nearly everything they did.

He convinced the Nephilim to attempt sexual unions with human women as well. The moment they entertained the thought and asserted their desire, the Nephilim began their fall to the temporal Earth. They discovered they were not only fertile with human women, but also with all forms of animal life. Their offspring were horribly twisted and grotesquely oversized for Earth life. Tribes of giant humans were formed very quickly. Some of the giants were retarded and had voracious appetites. They forced humans to be their slaves, feeding them and caring for them. Generation after generation, the blood of the Nephilim spread.

First generation offspring were almost like animals, devoid of compassion or consideration for any other life than their own. They were short lived and prone to debilitating arthritis and organ failure. They would wade into the sea and drown themselves rather than suffer as a crippled invalid. The next generation had more human features and desires. They could develop skills for fighting and for physical strategy. Within a few hundred generations, the pure seed of Adam was at risk of being bred out of existence. God's best creation was about to be wiped out through the lustful vengeance of Lucifer and his league of Nephilim.

This Earth, upon which Adam had been formed, was designed to couple with another Earth upon which lower man was already well developed. But, first, it had to be cleaned up. The genetic code needed to be purified again. The Flood was decided and the time for its application was set. For centuries, the giants pleaded with Enoch to be saved, to be preserved. For centuries, that answer was always the same. There was no ,and would never be an ability to save them. After 330 years, Enoch took his entire city and left the Earth. Another group left the Earth, knowing that their fall involved mortality, albeit they were virtually immortal. A few years later, Noah completed the ark, and that Earth was merged with the temporal Earth in orbit around a main sequence Sun on one of the outer belts of the Milky Way galaxy. The temporal planet, being constructed mostly of water, flooded them together and took more than seven months to settle.

When the ark came to rest, the seed of Eve walked into what was left of the existing race of man that had tilled the temporal Earth for millennia. Among the seed of Eve were the seed of Adam and the seed of Lucifer. Within a few years, the Nephilim returned to Earth. This time, they knew they could not breed with mankind. They would conquer them another way. They would use the greed and lust of men to accomplish their master's goal.

And when a man became humble, they would make him proud that he was humble. They would tempt him with more gold than any man could spend in a thousand lifetimes. They would provide sex slaves and soldiers and weapons more advanced than ever seen before. They would give them victory after victory and influence the elements so that even in games of chance, they would win. Even presidential elections would be decided with games of chance with every contest handed to the dark prince's disciple. With each victory, the commitment of that soul to the dark prince and his reward was made sure. One day, the evil support for that being would be taken from them, and they would be evil all by themselves. Then, would come the betrayal. It always came. Often, the sight of its approach was too great to behold, and they would take their own lives. They were led to believe that the overwhelming misery they felt as the betrayal robbed them of any pleasure their cars and planes, their private islands, and their stables of slave girls and boys brought them would end if they could only die.

The truth is that the misery remained and followed them to the realm of the dark prince, where all of his converts reside. And when a new body is offered to them, it is only through his seed, which although mortal, will never choose the light again. They will seek darkness and are promised rewards only if they die in battle as they try to kill all the other mortal infidels. It is how the dark prince achieves victory over the Creator.

And when a world is harvested through the separation of the Union of the Polarity, the souls left behind on the temporal planets are his for the taking. The misery of a world full of noxious weeds, biting insects, and a wilderness that must be beaten into submission is fully appreciated when you add the perpetual hatred for those who escaped onto a world like unto the Garden of Eden. The most powerful rage of regret comes only when that soul realizes that the choice between those worlds was theirs and theirs alone, and merely a change of heart away.

"You are a fool, General," said Semyaza. "The stars on your shoulder desecrate the rules of order by which you earned them. Mortals are like a small flame burning above a tiny sponge soaked with alcohol. You can cook a pot of soup with it. But, when you pour liquid oxygen over that flame, you can lift a rocket into space with it."

"Please enlighten me, my master," said the General.

"Let me make it simple for your tiny military brain," said Semyaza sarcastically. "Riker just poured pure oxygen over the entire Earth. The humans with any flame left will blaze with power."

"You know everything, master. How did Robert Riker, unknown to the world just a few months ago, walk into the world's most secure communications compound and make such a profound change?" asked Wes. General Morlay was an Air Force Academy graduate with a War College post graduate degree. He was a master tactician, but during the period of president Obama's sequestration, academy graduates were not immune from being fired, as they had been in years past. After 25 years of excellent service and the acquisition of his third star, he was introduced to Semyaza. Needless to say. All obstacles to his tenure and his utilization in the higher echelons of national defense were removed immediately.

After nearly 5 years at NORAD, his contributions enhanced the space-based surveillance and nuclear attack systems until they were fully operational. They had the ability to not only immediately detect the ignition of a rocket with a nuclear warhead, but to deliver a tactical nuclear warhead to the exact origin of that rocket within 60 seconds. The hint of this capability was demonstrated during the late 2016 launch of a North Korean attack on the United States disguised as a space flight test. The sea-based launch was obliterated with 2 minutes of the launch. The news media was told to report that it was a malfunction in the launch by the North Koreans. The rest of the military community knew it was the space-based NORAD attack program, although the State department maintained that NORAD was simply a training and simulation center.

Of course, Semyaza had been working with the North Koreans to make the launch happen in the first place. If the missile reached its target, he won. If the missile was destroyed and the launch site was nuked in retaliation, he won. The purpose of his duty on Earth was to keep the battles coming, without winning the war. In fact, if there was no declaration of war, it was even better for his purpose of economic enslavement of both countries. Every dollar spent on weapons was a dollar squeezed from the fruit of liberty in favor of security.

"You are clever for a human, General Morlay," began Semyaza in his usual complimentary tone. "There are certain juxtapositions in time from which an almost infinite number of pathways connect. The third full Moon of every year has its importance, as you might recall. The fourth new Moon at the end of the Age is paramount, because it begins the time of travail for the Earth. It is written that she is about to give birth, but by promising world leaders the power to levy a climate change tax, I convinced the masses that she was dying.

"I have also taught the religious leaders of this world that with every big change like this, as with every blessing, there must be a sacrifice of the same degree. There are nearly eight billion souls alive on the Earth right now. For this change, I will require at least half of the souls on Earth. We were on target to have well over that amount. There are only small pockets of resistance scattered around the globe. Or, so it was before Riker's broadcast." His tone changed to foreboding and almost threatening.

"The demise of planet Earth must take place in as much darkness as possible. But Riker's words, and they were astonishingly well arranged, has caused these pockets of light to begin coalescing. Soon, there will be strong connections between them, and a fabric will begin to form. If the Earth passes through the veil with this fabric intact, many thousands of years of focused effort on behalf of me and my team will have been thwarted. Do you understand me, General?"

"I believe so," said Wes Morlay, now slightly inflated with the notice paid to his genius. "The fever is always worse at night. Birth takes place only after the mother passes through a period of darkness to sever her child's spirit from its spirit home, locking it into the physical body until it dies. The darkness before dawn is as necessary as the pain of childbirth."

Although Nephilim are nearly 12 feet tall, they come with a variety of shapes and trim. Some have wings. Some have feathers, while still others are covered in smooth tiny scales. Some are quick and strong, while others are slender and articulate. Semyaza had a physical presence that was awesome to behold. He had a human shape to his head and face, with wide set eyes and a rather large nose. He had long, flowing blonde hair, but at the neck, his body was covered in short fine fur. His arms were very long and each hand had six fingers that were long and powerful. He has been the leader of the Nephilim here on the Earth since the Garden of Eden. He was once as good as ever there was an angel. And now, only the dark prince Lucifer was more evil.

"Truer words I have not heard from a human, I do believe," said Semyaza smoothly.
"I just want to make sure we are on the same page," said Wes.

"I just want to make sure we are on the same planet, General."

Chapter 32

"I wonder what time it is," asked Riker.

"My secret service watch says it's 10 PM," replied Bett with a distant voice. "It also says it's 50 degrees out here."

"Yeah, well my accu-window forecast says its dark as midnight out here, and we have a ways to walk if we can't hitch a ride. Any hope of reaching out to someone with that watch?"

"Oh. Well, I'm not sure. Let me press the button and try," she said. She lifted her wrist to her mouth, and pressed the button on the front. "Hello?"

"Bett is that you?" came Jones' voice back loud and clear.

"Oh my God. I am not believing this. Yes, it's me and the president. We're outside the access door at Camp David."

"Stay where you are. I will come to get you," replied Jones.

"Did you happen to mention it was cold out here?" asked Riker.

"Bob? Where do you think everyone went? I mean, there were bodies and blood everywhere, and then they were just gone," said Bett.

"Yes, I noticed that too. Someone cleaned up, but there were still bullet holes everywhere. I guess no one really talks about what goes on here."

"The whole mountain shook when Enoch had me break the sixth seal. That scared the hell out of me," said Riker.

"Yeah, well I think that's the idea," added Bett.

"I guess we'll find out soon what that really means," said Riker.

"I remember doing the time schedule research on the Union of the Polarity. The scripture says something about there being silence in Heaven for the period of about half an hour. But, who knew how to measure half an hour back then? Nobody, right? Then we proceeded with the assumption in mathematics that one day equals one thousand years. Our peer review accepted that assumption just fine. So, this means that half an hour in Heaven is 21 years on Earth. So, if my calculations are correct, and you just opened the sixth seal, then we have this period of time plus 21 years before the mountain on fire is cast into the sea."

"I am not a great scriptorian, but what is supposed to happen during this period just after the sixth seal?"

"Well, according to the records left by the ancients, there should be intense meteor showers, tidal waves, earthquakes, and volcanic eruptions that fill the atmosphere with particulate matter, which darkens the Sun and makes the Moon blood red. It will be a rough time to own beachfront property," said Bett.

"I don't really understand how raising one's frequency or giving off more light from our hearts is going to make a difference for people living east of Yellowstone, when that super volcano goes off," said Riker.

"Well, one thing is for sure, Mr. President, the powers that be didn't build enough of shelters like these for everyone. I suppose if you didn't get a ticket, you're going to be covered in dust like the people of Pompei or Harrapa."

"Harrapa? Where the hell is that?' asked Riker.

"Well, it's in Pakistan. The Indus Valley. Around 2,500 B.C. Harappa was wiped out in a nuclear blast. The soil was turned to glass. The explosion was the brightness of the sun. There was a pillar of smoke that rose to heaven. Sound familiar? So, who had nuclear weapons in those days and why use them against the Harappans? That's what I meant. Are we going to nuke eachother again?"

"Wow. I guess I needed to attend more history classes," said Riker.

"Well, sorry to say, you would not have learned any of this in any government school," quipped Bett.

"Hey. Headlights," said Riker.
"Should we hide?" asked Bett in a panic.

Riker pointed to her watch. "Call Jones"

"Oh yeah." She raised the watch. "Jones, are those your lights?"

"Roger that. Hang tight. Be there in a sec."

Within a minute, the white, 15 passenger van appeared beside them. Riker climbed in front, and Bett climbed in the first row in the back. The van was warm and welcome after the cold night air outside the mountain access door. "We're exhausted, Jones," said Riker.

"And we have a million questions for you," said Bett leaning forward as Jones turned the van around to drive back the way he had come. ""First of all, when we came out of the radio room, all the bodies were gone. Everyone was gone. Smith's body was gone."

"Well, last part first. Smith is a whole lot tougher than even I thought. He pulled through emergency surgery a couple of hours ago. He'll recover," said Jones as a matter of fact.

"I thought he was dead, for sure," said Bett about ready to cry again as she recalled in her mind his lightning fast reactions by jumping in front of a bullet for her.

"And what happened to General Cabarrus? I mean one second he was punching holes through the door with his gun, and the next second, everything went silent out there," asked Riker.

"Cabarrus didn't make it. Rhino hit him so hard, it killed him. The official story is, he died of a brain hemorrhage," said Jones.

"He's alive?" asked Bett again, just barely able to contain herself with tears. She could not tell what was happening inside of her. She was filled with joy that he did not die trying to protect her, but she was so close to bursting into tears all over again. She wrestled with these emotions she had never felt before.

"Yes. The indomitable agent Smith is alive. You'll see him in the morning."

"I guess that's my next question. Where are we going?" asked Riker.

"Those trailers we passed coming in earlier today? They're like a 4-star hotel of sorts. You both have quarters there. Safe, private, and never been used before," said Jones. "I guess it's still today," he said looking at his watch. "It's almost midnight."

"Feels like it's been a week," said Bett.

"I appreciate the quarters, but I really need to be heading back to Washington. What's happening out there?" asked Riker.

"I'm not the one to give you that information, Mr. President," said Jones. "The newsies are pretty much just talking about the EAS being activated during prime time. Fox News is trying to decipher the message, but the rest of them are upset that the EAS was abused for what they're reporting as a political Stunt."

"A what?" asked Riker in complete astonishment.

"You see? I can't be the one to brief you. Hadid is better at this. Besides, Orphan's father sent someone an hour ago that is tapped into everything. You'll see her in the morning."

"Her?"

"Yeah. And for a newspaper person, she is very fine, I might add," said Jones.

"Okay, G-man, what I want to know is do these hotel trailers have a buffet line?" asked Bett trying to regain her male dominant side, if just for a moment.

"Yes ma'am," said Jones knowing it irritated her. "John took care of that before he left."

"John left?" asked Riker.

"Yes, Mr. President. He said something about being needed elsewhere, and he would see us again in another place."

"That's exactly what Enoch said."

"Enoch" Where is he?" asked Jones.

"Like she said. He gave us some directions, and we left him back in Building E," said Riker.

"Another time and place, he said," Bett repeated distantly.

"There seems to be another layer to the Secret Service that I am not privy to," said Jones.

"You are more right than you know," said Riker.

"Hey, there are the trailers," perked up Bett. "I need a bathroom, guys."

"Yours is the last one down. I think you'll like it," said Jones. "John said everything you'll need is in there." Jones pulled up to the last trailer to let Bett out of the van. "We'll see you at zero eight hundred in the first trailer."

"Roger that," she said as she held her watch up to her mouth and pretended to talk into it. She hopped out of the van and bounded up the four stairs and disappeared behind the door.

"That girl has a strong personality," said Jones as be backed up to the second trailer.

"She has earned her right to be that way," said Riker.

"This trailer is the president's suite," said Jones. "We will be in the third trailer, right next door, if you need anything."

"You said Bayazed had sent someone?"

"Yes, Mr. President. She is in the last trailer with Bett. There are two rooms in that unit. By the way, breakfast is at zero seven thirty in the first trailer."

"Very good, agent Jones. I will see you at 8 in the morning," said Riker as he opened his door and slid to the ground. He closed the door of the van and said under his breath, "What a ride."

Rhino and Orphan were sharing football stories and Dick and Kyle were huddled around his laptop when Jones arrived back at trailer number three. "Guys, I don't want to play dad here, but breakfast is at zero seven thirty, and it's pushing zero one hundred now," he said looking at his watch.

"How is agent Smith," asked Orphan.

"He came out of surgery okay. He may be here in the morning. He's a tough guy," said Jones.

"He is da man, you know. I never seen a man move that fast before. He has reflexes like a Manu Alii, you know?" said Rhino.

"A manu what?" asked Kyle looking up from his laptop.

"A Manu Alii. It means in English, bird who walks like a chief. They are so fast on the ground, you cannot believe."

"That's very cool, Rhino. Very cool," said Dick.

"Well, no one will forget what you did today, my friend," said Jones. "You saved the president's life."

"I am sorry about that man. I didn't know what else to do," said Rhino.

"And don't forget making the couch into a bulldozer," said Dick as everyone laughed off the stress of those few minutes in a firefight.

"The importance of what we did today cannot be overemphasized. It isn't every day you get to save the world," said Jones.

"You mean A world," said Rhino. "One of the two worlds will not be saved today."

"Or maybe ever, if what I saw from that plane last night is a sample of what's to come," said Dick.

"Let me tell you. I saw the power of these frequencies Rhino was talking about this afternoon. We lost 11 men on that rig, and spilled oil from here to kingdom come," said Orphan.

"It is some major high strangeness that we all met the way we did. I mean, we have really affected everything today," said Kyle.

"Hah! Like Yuki would say, 'I like the way you say strangeness'," said Dick.

"Yeah, exactly," responded Kyle.

"Well, like I said," said Jones standing up from the arm of the couch in the common area of the dorm trailer, "You better get some rack time. Zero seven thirty comes on

186

Eastern time around here," he said pointing at each of them, knowing they were all from California.

"Yeah. I'm pretty beat," said Orphan. "I'm crashing."

"Hopefully, I am not crashing," said Dick. "I'll see you all in the morning.

"There is a set of showers down the hall. There are three sizes of jumpsuits in the closet there, in case you want to change out of your civies and dress in some official government threads," said Jones.

"Can we keep it?" asked Kyle.

"You wear it, you keep it," said Jones.

"You got one my size?" asked Rhino.

"Um, maybe not. You are the man, remember?" responded Jones. He smiled and put his hand on Rhino's shoulder as a congratulations for a job well done. "We have some pretty good resources, Mr. Rhino. Don't worry."

Chapter 33

Bett walked into the last trailer in the little village made deep in the woods on Camp David. The door opened into a living room setting with very nice furniture. There was a small stack of squares where people would leave their shoes. She obliged and took off her black combat style boots. Her jeans were long enough to drag the floor, when she wasn't wearing those boots, so she bent over to put a cuff in each leg to keep from stepping on them with her heels. She felt sore, and it was no wonder. She thought about the events of the last 36 hours. Her heart was sore from the stress of the battle inside Building E.

She looked up from her cuffing, and noticed there was a woman sitting in one of the light green overstuffed chairs in the living room. The beautifully shaded lamp was on a small early American end table between the chair and a matching couch. "Oh, Hi. I'm Bett Dyson," she said walking toward the woman in long strides with her right hand stretched out.

Standing up and taking one step forward, the woman said in a soft and very clean voice, "I'm Shelly. Shelly Lasalle. KTLA news. Well, I was as of yesterday before this call."

"The news, huh? You a reporter?" asked Bett, shaking her hand firmly.

"Well, not exactly. Not this time, I mean. My boss, my benefactor, Mr. Bayazed, sent me. I'm here to help get the story out."

"The story? " asked Bett worried about the details of the firefight coming out. Rhino had killed a man. Smith had been shot. The president had sent out a broadcast that she could only vaguely recall, as she was in a state of extreme grief.

"Mr. Bayazed wanted to make sure the Emergency Access System broadcast reached everyone on the planet. My crew and I saw you guys almost get killed in Victorville, as

188

it turns out." She said as she brought her hands together in front of her folded, and then unfolded.

"Oh, you were in the news helicopter we almost..."

"Yes. Our pilot, Elvis, knew exactly what to do, but we saw the missiles," interrupted Shelly.

"That was close, and I swear I thought the wings were coming off," said Bett.

"Elvis said he never saw a jet do that before," said Shelly twisting her right hand in the air over her head.

"Oh. Yeah, we had this super hacker named Kyle who made up this special gas of some kind. Him and Dick Daring mounted these fuel bottles in the cargo bay. It was like rocket fuel or something, because we escaped those missiles at over the speed of sound flying all the way out into space. We were weightless," said Bett.

"Yeah," she said now knowing that the purple Dodge and the fast black helicopter were also involved in this amazing adventure. "You see, that is the story that I am supposed to capture. Something is happening, and it's really big. There have been earthquakes, volcanoes, and then the president's broadcast to the world. Mr. Bayazed sent me here to get that story and tell it to the world. He knows something ancient is at play, but this is the twenty first century, and people don't believe in that stuff anymore. He wants everyone to know what is a stake, and what they can do about it. He said I am like a scribe."

"Well, you are very beautiful for a scribe," said Bett.

"Thank you," said Shelly with a genuine humility.

"I mean it," she paused. Bett felt somehow out of place in this incredibly fine living space with Shelly showing that a beautiful woman could also be successful. "Listen, Jones told me that breakfast is at seven thirty AM, and I am totally wiped."

"Oh, yeah. I almost forgot. You're professor, Doctor..."

"Wesson? She's here?"

"Yes. She went to bed earlier. She said if you need anything at all to call the number by your phone in your room. There is someone there twenty four hours a day, and they are like a concierge on steroids. Your room is the first one on the right down the hall."

"Oh my god. That is perfect. I just realized that there is something I need, like before morning. Thank you. I will see you in the morning,"

"Shelly," said Shelly smiling.

"Yes. Shelly. I'm not so good with names. I'm getting better, though. Thanks," said Bett walking down the hall to her room. Within a few seconds she opened the door and walked into the room flipping the light switch on the wall. "Oh my god," she said quietly as she closed the door behind her. "Talk about the Ritz."

She picked up the phone and put it to her ear. There was a dial tone. She dialed the number on the postit note.

"Good evening, Camp David service. How can I help you?" asked the pleasant female voice. Young and professional, thought Bett.

"Yes. This is Bett Dyson, and I'm staying at one of the trailers at Camp David. Oh, sorry. I just realized I don't even know the room number or anything."

"That's okay, Miss Dyson. I can tell by the call board exactly where you are. What can I do for you?"

Miss Dyson? She hadn't heard that term in years. "Um, yes. Well, I need to know if you can find me a really nice dress."

Chapter 34

There was a soft knock at the door. "Mr. President, it is time," said Hadid softly through the door of the presidential suite bedroom.

"Okay. I'm up," said Riker. He wasn't, but the routine time for getting up was six AM anyway. Regardless of the previous three days of incredible activities, and the dreams scattered through the night, he felt fairly well rested. "Wow," he said as he walked into the bathroom shower area. "No wonder the defense budget is always so high," he said under his breath. Within a few minutes he had showered and shaved and opened the closet to find a crisp, dark blue jumpsuit with the presidential emblem above the left breast pocket. "Well, this is one day I welcome not having to wear a suit."

Riker exited the presidential trailer and was strangely in awe at the beauty of this place. The pine trees were about 150 feet tall and densely spaced all around the small pad where the trailers were set up. Such a contrast in this spot, he thought. There was a morning breeze, but it was high in the trees making a muffled sawing sound that seemed to come from everywhere. He was reminded of something Enoch had said about God's voice making the sound of rushing waters. The sunlight pierced through the upper branches through the slightly misty air to the needle covered forest floor. He breathed deeply through his nose and could smell the fragrance of pine trees and spring blossoms somewhere on the mountain nearby. He could hear blue jays and magpies vying for mates in the trees. Truly, this was a phenomenal planet, he thought. "The great and terrible day of the Lord is perhaps not today," he said to himself as he walked slowly toward the first trailer.

"Good morning, Mr. President," said Orphan now walking up behind him from the third trailer.

"Oh, good morning, Orphan. Sleep okay?"

"Yes sir. That was the nicest room I have seen in a long time; well, since home," he said with a tender sound to his voice.

"Hey, you have been through some amazing things for a man your age. I have a feeling you're set up to do great things."

"Yeah. I mean yes sir. That is what my father says. 'Always set your sights on doing great things.'"

"I got the same message from my wife. She was amazing. I think the Earth is trying to tell us that time is no longer a luxury. Let's get something to eat, what do you say?" said Riker.

"That sounds great," said Orphan.

"Oh, good morning," said Loretta as she walked into the plush living room area of the trailer.

"Good morning, Dr. Wesson," said Shelly.

"Have you seen Bett?" asked Loretta.

"Yes, I met her last night. She is still in her room. First one on the right," she said pointing without raising her arm.

Loretta walked back down the hall and knocked softly on the door. "Bett, are you awake?"

"Yes, but I am not ready to come out yet. You two go on ahead, and I'll catch up in a few," said Bett from behind the door.

"Okay. See you at breakfast." She walked back to the living room area and without sitting down, said, "Well, shall we? West coast time is a drag, and I need some coffee. You?"

"Oh yes," said Shelly. As they opened the door, they both stopped on the small deck just outside. "Wow."

"I know what you mean. You don't see mornings like this in California, do you?" said Loretta.

"I guess the president needs a nice place to get away from the Washington slime pit from time to time. No wonder presidents since Truman have been coming here," said Shelly.

"I wonder if they rent this place out. Listen to that wind up there," said Loretta craning her head back to find only a small amount of blue sky through the tall pines. "Well, let's go. I think I smell coffee."

Dick opened his eye, amazed to see the light glow of sunlight coming through the curtained window. "Well, that was nice," he said under his breath. His pillow was dry. He had not crashed. Peace filled his soul like nothing he had ever felt before. It was like a burden he had carried for so long, never knowing when it was going to send his heart racing and his mind into a cloud of panic. It had been lifted from him as he had wrestled that jet through the upper atmosphere. It seemed like his whole life had been forged through a refiner's fire for one event that might save the world. "Oh, seven fifteen. Shower," said Dick to himself hopping out of the brand new bed and onto the perfect carpet. He grabbed a bathrobe out of the closet and headed to the common bathroom of the dorm trailer.

Two doors down, and he swung open the door to the common bathroom. "Holy crap," he said.
"I know, right?" said Kyle already out of the shower and zipping up his jumpsuit. "Like the Hilton."
"Hilton, shit. This is like Trump Tower presidential.
"There are new tooth brushes and toothpaste, body soap and shampoo in this drawer," said Kyle. "Have at it. I'll meet you in the living room in twenty."
"Sure thing. Hey, you seen the others?" asked Dick.
"Rhino and Orphan? I know Orphan left for breakfast at around seven fifteen. I haven't seen Rhino yet."
"Okay. See you in a few."

Kyle walked back up the hallway to the living room area of the dorm trailer. "Whoa, dude. Looking very fine," said Kyle. Rhino was standing in the living room looking out the window. He was wearing a dark blue jumpsuit with an emblem over the left breast pocket.

"Yeah. It fits, amazingly. Some lady brought it by at six thirty this morning with Jones. I don't think that guy ever sleeps," said Rhino. "Those showers are all pro, don't you think?"

"Brass and marble and class, that's for sure," said Kyle.

"Sleep good?"

"Like I hadn't slept in a week."

"Is Mr. Daring coming?"

"Oh, it's just Dick. Women call him Daring Dick. Something about racecar drivers with a patch over one eye, I don't know."

"So you guys really race on the street?

"Yeah. Street racing for money put up by gambling addicts the world over. They love the real thing. Loud and dangerous. Well, and Yuki," said Kyle.

"Yuki?"

"Oh yeah. She's an ultra hot Japanese genius that built the idea into a righteous endeavor that pays to play. I do the software engineering."

"You're a hacker?"

"At your service," said Kyle, as he twisted the door knob on the front door and stepped out onto the deck. "Now, this is freedom," he said into the cool morning air.

Rhino ducked down and stepped through the doorway onto the deck. "I have never seen anything like this before. Heaven could have nothing on this place."

"I know what you mean. God can do some major graphics."

"Smell the pines?"

"Makes you never want to go back to the smog alerts of socal, eh?"

"I think about everything that has happened. How many turns my life has taken that brought me here, to the president's back yard. I am an expert at physical chemistry and statistics, but I still don't know how I got here."

"It's random, my friend."

"No, it's not. Time isn't like that. From a photon's point of view, the entire universe is local. You know the equation, E equals M C squared, right?"

"Yeah. Einstein. Atomic bomb. Nasty math."

"Well, it shows the relationship between time and speed," said Rhino. "Space is not measured in distance. It is measured in terms of time; you know, light years. The closer you come to the speed of light, mass become infinite. In others words, distance approaches zero. Time approaches zero. The past, the present, and the future, all visible from one place. The faster we go, the more we can see," he said spreading his arms wide to encompass the whole forest they could see from the deck.

"Like God? Omniscient?"

"Like God. Not God, but like Him. I think that is what He meant," said Rhino as thought he just now got it.

"Meant what?"

"He said that we would know Him when He comes, because we will be like Him," said Rhino. "We will be able to see everything, just like He does."

"Very intense, bro. Right now, I am seeing breakfast in the very near future," said Kyle trying to lighten things up a little.

"Me too. You know we had no dinner last night. I think I'm wasting away here."

"Yeah all three the both of us. Hey, where's Dick?"

"I'm right here," said Dick dragging a comb through his jet black hair.

"Nice jumpsuit," said Kyle.

"I got the memo. Hey, very nice dark blue, my friend. How do you rate?"

"They brought me one the right size this morning. Jones said they have resources. Yours is light blue and mine is dark blue."

"Rank has its privilege," said Kyle.

"I think it's more like 'size matters' buddy," said Dick offering a fist bump to Rhino, who acknowledged it with his enormous, smooth brown hand. "Hey, has anyone checked out this awesome scenery?"

"I know, right?" said Kyle.

"Let's go. I like my omelets a certain way," said Dick.

They walked down the wooden steps to the newly paved pad on which the trailers were placed. They walked side by side past the second trailer to the first. They were quiet at first, breathing in the misty forest air, like they wanted this stroll to last for hours. As they made the turn around the second trailer, with the warm sun blades slicing through the scene over the right shoulder, they saw a man in a suit, sitting in a wheelchair a dozen yards ahead of them.

"Smith," said Dick.

They each quickened their pace a little to reach him. "Good morning, gentlemen," said Smith.

"Good morning. Shit. Great morning. I am so glad you made it," said Dick with all the sincerity he could muster.

"You da man, like no other," said Rhino reaching out with his left hand, as he noticed Smith's right arm was in a sling. Smith shook it firmly and looked him the eye. "I thought you took the final round," said Rhino with a softness to his voice.

"Me too," said Smith.

"We're the last ones, aren't we?" asked Dick.

"No. There is one more," said Smith.

"Oh. Yeah. Let's go guys. We'll see you inside?"

"Yes. No worries, guys. I will be along in a few. Could you send Jones out here when you see him?"

"Sure thing," said Dick.

They walked up the gently sloped ramp into the double glass doors of the dining hall first trailer. The smell of bacon and coffee was amazing.

"Good morning, team. Wow. Look at those jumpsuits," said Riker.

"You gonna be on the team, you gotta look like a player," said Rhino.

"This will look great with my black Honda wrapped around it," said Dick.

"I don't know. Shelly tells me you have a pretty badass Dodge," said Riker.

Dick's face got red for a moment. "Don't look at me. He's the one that makes it go fast," said Dick pointing at Kyle.

"Better living through chemicals I always say," said Kyle.

"Yeah, how does she know anyway?" asked Dick.

"I was in the news helicopter you left in the dust on the foothill freeway," said Shelly.

"Oh yeah. Well imagine the look on the police helicopter pilot's face," trailed Dick.

"Dude. That's right. There is a warrant for us back in Cali," said Kyle.

"Oh yeah. Can anyone fix a ticket around here?" asked Dick with a smile on his face.

The whole room erupted in laughter. "Oh yeah, Jones. Smith wanted me to tell you he needs you outside," said Dick.

"Thanks," said Jones as he began walking toward the doors.

"Hey, where's Bett?" asked Rhino.

"She will be along in a minute," said Loretta. "She said she didn't feel like breakfast."

"Well, I do," said Rhino.

"Yeah. Can they make custom omelets at this place?" asked Dick.

"There is a chef around the corner there. Anything you like, boys. Also, coffee is self pour right over there against the wall. Fresh, too. Not instant," said Riker. "Hadid, can you just show them where everything is? Thanks."

Hadid nodded politely and followed the three men over to the grill, where a short, round man in a white chef's uniform and a stiff white hat waited with a smile.

Jones walked through the swinging glass doors of the dining hall trailer and down the ramp to the asphalt pad where Smith was seated in his wheelchair. "You okay?' he asked.

"Yeah. Just can't get enough of this morning," said Smith.

"I know what you mean."

Jones stood there at the side of Smith in silence. They had been professionals assigned only to presidential duties for almost five years. They had been through protests, bank failures, parades, and elections. They had been punched, kicked, spat upon, and called names by first ladies that ladies should never use. They knew secrets that could land officials in prison, but they always kept the secrets. They could keep their faces from talking. In all of those years and with all of those challenges, came a bond of friendship that only soldiers in the field know. Brothers could feel what brothers felt. "She'll be along," he said.

"Yeah. If you could just, you know," said Smith.

"This time, I must respectfully decline. You gotta do this on your own, my brother," said Jones. And with that, he turned slowly and walked back into the dining hall.

Smith had been married to his job for so long. A woman would have been, hell had been a complication in his life. They didn't punch a clock, like most jobs. If the president was up, they were up. If he flew somewhere, they were in a corner watching. Congressman would throw things and curse and threaten, but Smith was only an elbow away should someone try to actually touch the president. There was no time to glance away at a cell phone or think about a woman who felt he wasn't spending enough time with her. But this was different. She hated him. She slapped him and poked him and yelled at him, but his heart was all the time hearing something different. He didn't know. He could think.

And, now, here he was sitting in a wheelchair he didn't need, outside in the cool parking lot waiting for that same person to come walking around the corner.

And then, as though he had just wished it, he saw her. Well, it was her, but it wasn't her. She was tall. No, she was taller. She was wearing heels. And slipped into those heels were beautiful, slender legs holding up a flowing dress that reached almost to her knees. It was her. The long strides, confident and motivated, floated her shape through the air while the sun flashed her beautiful blonde hair each time she passed through a shard of its golden warmth. Her dark eyes were fixed in one place, straight ahead. They did not blink, but were focused as though she was about to let go an arrow at the target sitting in a wheelchair not far away.

His heart was flying, because he could never imagine himself kissing this woman. But he did imagine it. She was true to the bone and required truth from her life. And she was looking at him. And he was looking at her. He tried to stand as she approached him. Something told him to stand up and face the challenge. But, for some reason his legs could not lift him. They were soft and used to sitting in the chair this morning. He slid forward in the chair, lifting the foot rests away so he could stand on the pavement.

But it was too late. She stopped in front of him like an ocean wave crashing on the rocks at his feet. She reached down with her hands and slid them under the lapels of his suit. And then without hesitation, she gripped those lapels and lifted him, it seemed, off the wheelchair seat and up into her lips. He reach around her waist with his powerful left arm and placed his hand flat on her spine. He gently pulled her into his warmth and kissed her back with every ounce of his soul. He felt her exhale and then breathe in deeply. He could feel her heart beating against his chest. Hers too, he thought.

In a few moments, matched only by those enjoyed by the trees covering them this morning, the kiss was over. They had said everything they needed to. He had changed for her. She had changed for him. Until the end of time, they both knew they would never part again.

"Coffee?" said Smith.
"Hell yes," said Bett.
"Give me a hand up the ramp?" he asked.
"I will if you tell me your first name."

The End

Stay tuned for Volume Two and Three.

Made in the USA
Charleston, SC
02 February 2017